Talk Me Down From The Edge

by Jade Winters

In loving memory of my Dad...

As the street lights mingled with the last dregs of day, David hurried along the wide tree-lined street. He was eager to get home. Ever since he had become a full time partner at Withers and Peterson Solicitors, arriving home before dark had been a rarity. He stopped outside a sizeable Edwardian house, the front lawn manicured to near perfection, surrounded by a cavalcade of chrysanthemums in spectacular bloom. As he started along the path towards the house, he rummaged in his jacket pocket searching for his keys. Finally locating them, he inserted the key into the lock and pushed the door open, stepping over the threshold into a spacious hallway.

'I'm home,' he called out as he shook off his jacket and hung it on the coat rail. He placed his briefcase on the floor next to the telephone table. He could suddenly hear the faint pitter-patter of feet advancing towards him.

'Dad!' Emily squealed as she rounded the corner and ran straight for him, nearly slipping on the polished oak floor.

He bent down and hugged her tightly. 'Hello squirt,' he said, as she looped her arms around his neck.

'You're home early,' she said excitedly.

'Told you I would be, didn't I?' he said as they walked along the high ceilinged hall and into the brightly decorated living room.

'Hi Dad,' James said coolly, barely looking up from his Xbox game. At ten, he was treading the fine line between childhood and soon-to-be moody teenager. A fact that was, at times, more evident than others. David rustled his hair with his spare hand and headed towards the sofa where his wife Laura sat.

'Hello gorgeous,' he said with a wink and flopped down next to her, out stretching his long legs.

'Hello yourself,' she said leaning towards him and planting a kiss firmly on his lips. Laura's sandy brown hair fell down on her neck in the frailest of ringlets; her adoring green eyes met his. 'Good day?' she enquired.

'So so,' he said. His strong lean face looking weary.

'Dad,' Emily said slyly as she squeezed her small frame between them, turning to look at her father to ensure she had his full attention.

'Yes Emily?' he replied. He wondered what she was after. Emily could wrap him around her little finger and he indulged her with great pleasure, *most of the time*.

'What are the chances of me getting a puppy for Christmas?' She looked up at him, her eyes glowing like gems. Her hair, the same colour as her mother's cascaded over her shoulders.

'I don't think Ninja would be too happy darling,' he said looking at Laura, 'what do you think?'

Putting a hand to Emily's cheek she said, 'I think, we've had this conversation before and we agreed that it wouldn't be kind to bring a dog into a home where a cat lives.'

'But Ninja is hardly in,' Emily challenged, 'and when he is, all he does is sleep - he never plays with me,' she said sulkily.

'That's what cats do silly,' James said as he paused his game and turned his attention to her, his sky coloured eyes mocking her. 'Animals are not toys for your entertainment.'

Laura looked at her son, impressed by his sensitive nature. It was something that she adored about him.

'I wasn't asking you,' Emily said huffily, moving to the single armchair.

'No, but he has a point,' Laura said, leaning back into David's arms.

Emily stared daggers at James who returned her stare with a look of smugness.

'I'll start dinner before world war three starts,' Laura said with a chuckle as she attempted to get up.

'No,' David said playfully, 'stay here.' He pulled her back into his arms. 'Why don't we eat out tonight, what'd you say Em?'

Emily refused to meet his gaze, looking out of the window instead.

'When does anything I say matter?' she asked with a pout.

'Em, that's not fair,' he replied. 'What you say matters loads - both of you - but when it comes to things like getting a dog, that decision will lay with your mother and I since it would be our responsibility.'

'But I would look after him,' she turned to look at him in the hope she could still persuade him.

'Okay, let me play devil's advocate,' he said. 'What happens to this imaginary dog when you're at school or when you want to hang out with your mates?'

'And boys,' James interjected, attempting to wind her up. She poked her tongue out at him, but said nothing to her father.

'James...' David said to his son, glancing at him - his eyes giving a subtle warning. He turned his attention back to Emily. 'Dogs are great responsibilities that need a lot of care and attention Em, and I don't think at this moment in time getting a dog is such a good idea. You say that you'll take care of him, but will that be so once he's here? Or will your mother and I end up being the ones feeding him and taking him for walks?'

Noting that he said "at this moment in time", Emily jumped at the opening. 'So we could get a dog sometime in the future?' she asked hopefully.

Laura tried to conceal her smile. David had walked straight into that one and as a solicitor should have been more selective with his choice of words.

'Maybe,' he said treading carefully, 'we'll see in a few years.'

Satisfied, she smiled at him, and then it was her turn to look smugly at James.

'Won't happen,' James mouthed at her, then resumed playing his game.

'Okay, enough talk about animals,' Laura said. 'Let's decide where we're going to eat.'

It was common practice when they were dining out, for each of them to write down the restaurant of their choice on a piece of paper and either James or Emily would pick the winner out of a bowl.

'It's my turn today,' Emily declared after the bowl had the four balls of paper in it. She squeezed her eyes shut and using two fingers picked out the paper. Opening it quickly, she squealed with delight. 'My choice,' she boasted, 'pizza.'

'Yum yum,' David said, 'pizza it is.' He stood up and held his hand out for Laura.

'Go and get your coats on,' she said taking his hand and heaving her up. Emily and James ran out of the living room and thundered up the stairs.

'Do those two walk anywhere?' David asked Laura half-joking, as he wrapped his arms around her.

'Nope,' she said looking up at him. Rich blondish-brown hair surrounded his lean intelligent face. 'Are you sure you're up for going out, you look tired, I can always run you a hot bath and bring dinner up to you,' Laura suggested. She hated seeing him like this.

He rested his forehead against hers. 'I got some bad news about a case today and it's kind of getting to me.' He sighed.

'Do you want to talk about it?' she asked, looking worried.

He looked at her tenderly. 'Maybe later,' he replied.

Laura's brow furrowed.

'You don't have to tell me all the details,' she assured him, 'I just don't think you should have to keep things bottled up inside all the time.'

'Ready!' they heard the children calling from the front door.

'I know, I just don't want to burden you with any unnecessary stress, I know what a delicate flower you are,' he said winking at her. 'Come on, let's go.' He held her hand and led her to the door.

A black shadow rushed through as they attempted to leave, nearly tripping James. Ninja had decided to come in for the night.

'A dog wouldn't do that!' Emily exclaimed, still trying to make her case.

'Enough, Em. The discussion is over,' David said as they walked to the car.

The local pizza restaurant was an eye-catching slightly upscale place with a broader menu than other pizza places. For this reason, it was always full.

A young buxom girl with bright red hair and a cheery face greeted them at the door.

'Good evening,' she said, 'I'm afraid there's a twenty minute wait for a table this evening, would you like to relax in the bar and I'll call you when your table is ready?'

'That would be great, thanks,' David said as he gave the waitress his name and led his family through to the bar. James and Emily headed straight for the video game machine whilst David ordered drinks for himself and Laura.

'So is Joe working this case with you?' she asked as she sipped her soft drink. She had opted to drive for the evening so David could drink and relax.

'No,' he answered, wincing as he experienced a sharp pain in his stomach.

'Are you okay?' Laura asked concern in her eyes.

'Yes fine,' he said as the pain receded. 'Probably doesn't help with me drinking too many of these,' he said raising his whiskey glass in mid-air before drinking the last remains and ordering another one. 'I think I have a serious case of acid. Either that or an ulcer!'

His glance fell on James who was energetically killing all the bad people in the virtual reality game he was playing whilst Emily looked on, admiring his obvious skill. They sat quietly for a moment, sipping their drinks, David in a world of his own.

Finally, Laura broke the silence. 'So,' she said, looking into her husband's eyes, 'tell all.' She was eager to find out what was troubling him.

David took a deep breath. 'A young boy - well he's eighteen, but looks much younger, has been charged with manslaughter for stabbing his stepfather.'

Laura raised her eyebrow in surprise. 'And you don't think he should have been?' she asked, trying to understand.

'It's not that clear cut,' David continued, 'there's a long history of abuse in the family, seems the stepfather went one beating too far and the boy just flipped, stabbed him thirty nine times in his legs,' he said, pausing to sip his drink. 'By some miracle he survived but was left paralysed from the waist down. Just when we thought it couldn't get any worse, he died this morning from a blood clot. We were informed that this was due to the injuries he sustained.'

'Oh that's terrible.'

'Yep, I'm going to try and appeal to the court for leniency. This kid has been abused since he was five, yet when he stands up for himself he's the one that is punished. It's cases like this that makes me want to chuck it all in,' he said, a tone of sorrow in his voice.

'Sometimes I wish you would, it's so emotionally draining for you,' she said, placing her hand over his.

'It helps having you and the kids to come home to. Without you, I don't know if I could do it.' He squeezed her hand. Laura blushed. They had been together for years, but he still made her melt.

'Well it's a good thing you have nothing to worry about on that score,' she said smiling, 'I will be with you forever.'

'And I with you,' he said lifting his glass up to her.

The evening out had done David the world of good. He consumed several more whiskeys, and was able to forget about the impending case and concentrate on his family. They ate more pizza than they should have and all declined the delicious desserts that were offered on the menu because of it. On the way home, Laura stopped at the local video shop and hired a family movie for the evening. *It's a perfect way to finish a perfect evening,* Laura thought to herself as she slipped the DVD into the player and joined her family on the sofa.

2

Eight had been a terrifying age for Laura. It was the year life had unveiled itself to her. It had been indifferent to her age, her wants or needs, when like a thief in the night it had stolen her father; in a blink of an eye, he was gone.

'Come on,' her tear stained mother coaxed her, 'you need to get out of this room, you can't stay in here forever,' she said, despite wishing she herself could crawl into her own bed and never get up.

'No,' Laura said stubbornly, 'I won't.' She pulled the covers over her head.

'Darling, the priest is downstairs and he would like to speak to you,' she said, her voice gentle and soothing.

'Tell him to go away. I don't believe him anymore! God doesn't love me, he doesn't love anybody! If he did he wouldn't have taken my dad away,' she cried, her body shuddering with every sob.

Her mother's gaze fell upon the picture frame on the bedside table; Greg, full of youth and vitality, holding an innocent smiling Laura in his arms. She blinked back the tears that blinded her grey eyes.

'Patricia,' a tentative voice called from below, 'visitors are arriving.'

She heard the front door being opened and the voices of women talking animatedly, albeit in hushed tones. Several seconds later, silence descended on the house again as the women were ushered into the living room.

'Laura, I'm going to have to go downstairs. Are you sure you don't want to come with me? Company might help get your mind off things.' Her question was met with muffled weeping. Without saying a word, she knew exactly what the answer was.

'Okay sweetheart, if you need me, just call,' her slender, dark-haired mother said, gently closing the door behind her.

Hearing her mother's footsteps descend the stairs, Laura lifted her head from beneath the covers. She rubbed her eyes, trying to correct her vision that was blurred with tears as she took the photograph that had meant so much to her and placed it against her chest. There was a gentle tap at the door. Before she could escape back under the covers, the door opened and Sarah, her best friend, stood at the entrance. Dressed from top to toe in black, she could have easily been mistaken for having just come from a funeral.

'Do you mind if I come in?' she asked with slight hesitation.

Laura shook her head, still clutching the precious frame in her hand.

Sarah took off her coat and sat on the bottom of the bed. A brief moment of awkward silence ensued before Sarah piped up, 'Father Donnelly is downstairs.'

Laura shrugged her shoulders. Father Donnelly had suddenly gone from someone Laura believed in and looked up to, to nothing more than a storyteller. Admittedly, he was quite the raconteur, but the tales he told were now nothing but fiction in her mind.

'He said that your dad is at peace now and is up there,' she said pointing upwards.

'How would he know?' Laura asked her, turning more bitter as the seconds ticked on.

'I don't know, but I remember him saying stuff like that when my mum died,' Sarah said, tears filling her own eyes.

Laura put the frame back on the table gently, crawled to the bottom of the bed and held Sarah's hand.

'It's okay though,' Sarah continued bravely,

'because Father Donnelly said we'll all see each other again... even Sandy is up there,' she said, smiling as she thought of her old German Shepherd dog.

Laura did not say anything else about her own shattered illusions of life in the sky. She did not want to upset Sarah.

'Why don't they ever say goodbye?' Laura asked suddenly. 'Why do they just go away? Do you think it's because they don't love us?'

'No,' Sarah said thoughtfully, 'Father Donnelly says that God has work for them to do so he calls them home.'

'Do you believe him?' Laura asked.

'I don't know, but I hope he isn't making my mum work too hard, she was always so tired before she went,' she said her bottom lip trembling.

They heard the front door slam shut then the soft padding of footsteps slowly mounting the stairs. They came to an abrupt halt as they reached Laura's door, then carried on walking further down the hallway.

***

The years following her father's death were tumultuous at best. Laura would never have got through them without Sarah's support. The depression her mother suffered had made it impossible for them to carry on as a normal family. Sarah remained at her side throughout all the vicissitudes of life.

'I just can't believe she wants to marry someone else and move to Australia, it's like she's forgotten all about Dad,' Laura cried like a spoilt child.

'Laura, it has been quite a few years,' Sarah said as they both sat on her bed. She lit a cigarette, trying to appear grown up. She took a drag and started to cough.

'Oh, put that out Sarah, you look very silly. I can't

understand why you think you look good inhaling smoke; you may as well go and put your lips around an exhaust pipe.'

'You're just out of date,' she said trying it again, inhaling a lesser amount. 'All famous people smoke.'

'Then they're idiots as well,' Laura said, still annoyed as she moved her hands to waft the smoke away from her face. 'Anyway getting back to what's important,' she snapped.

At seventeen, both girls were quite the opposite of one another. Whilst Laura was serious and studious, Sarah was a free spirit, refusing to be bogged down by anything. She liked to live in the moment.

'When my dad married the witch, I was just happy to see a smile on his face again. God - I don't think he smiled for years after my mum died; it was like growing up in the dark. I'm surprised I turned out as well balanced as I have,' she said.

Laura laughed. 'If you're well balanced, I'd hate to see what an unbalanced person looks like.'

'Hey you!' Sarah said slapping her arm jokingly. 'Seriously though, just be happy for your mum, she's been on her own for such a long time, it can't be nice not having a boyfriend,' she said. 'I know I'd go insane if I didn't have one.' She took another small puff, flopped back on the bed and stared distantly at the ceiling.

'And how is boring Pete?' Laura enquired, lying down beside her.

'Boring!' Sarah laughed. 'Trying to get any action out of him is like trying to revive a corpse. He's definitely got to go.'

'Will you ever be content?' she asked her.

'Only when I'm dead,' she said as she practised blowing hoops with the cigarette smoke.

'The smell of that is making me feel sick,' Laura said as she reached over to open the window. 'I need some fresh air.' She snatched the cigarette out of Sarah's hand and threw it out.

Sarah gasped jokingly. 'Litter bug!' she yelled whilst laughing.

It hadn't taken Laura long to realise that Sarah was right about her mother. She had finally given her blessing, though she was heartbroken when the time came for her to leave. She had driven her mother and stepfather to the airport on the day of their departure.

'I'm sorry things have turned out this way,' Patricia said, tears freely flowing down her face. 'You do know I love you, don't you?' she asked, her eyes searching Laura's face.

'Of course I do,' she reassured her. 'You're doing the right thing Mum, and anyway I would have had to be on my own sooner or later.'

'You're sure you'll be alright? You know you are welcome to come.'

'Mum, I'm going to be living with Sarah, how could it not be alright?' she said squeezing her hand.

Her mother couldn't argue with that. She had to face the fact that Sarah had been Laura's support system when she herself couldn't be.

'You two will always be inseparable,' she predicted.

The two women embraced and reluctantly let go. Laura watched as her mother's small frame disappeared through the departures door. Sarah was all she had left.

***

The merciless sun blared down on their bikini-clad bodies. The air was hot and humid. Laura sat up, unable to bear the heat any longer.

'I'm going in for a dip,' she said as she stood up and brushed the golden sand from her body. At nineteen, her body had filled out and the once flat-chested girl had blossomed into a well-developed young woman.

'Rather you than me,' Sarah said looking up at her, shielding the sun from her eyes with her hand.

'I'll burn to death if I lay in the sun for one more second,' she said as she walked towards the sea, careful to avoid stepping on the sun-baked bodies littering the sand.

She eased herself into the cool water and closed her eyes. One minute she was enjoying the tranquil waves washing over her, the next she was making a futile attempt to get her footing and composure as a rip current tugged at her ankles, knocking her off balance and pulling her away from the shore. Unwillingly, Laura succumbed to the pull of the invisible predator under the waves. Panicking, she felt for the floor beneath her, desperately trying to dig her fingers into the seabed, attempting to crawl back to the seashore, but to no avail – the water violently wrenched her weakening body one way, then the other, as though she was merely a rag doll. She tried screaming but warm salty seawater engulfed her open mouth, muffling her frantic pleas for help and her lungs ached. As she closed her eyes, finally surrendering to the moment, she suddenly felt a hand roughly yank her arm, pulling her body up into fresh air.

'Are you okay?' the bare-chested stranger asked, trying to control her flailing arms.

'Yes, I think so,' she said coughing up the last remains of water from her chest and inhaling deeply.

'Let's get you back to shore,' he said, putting his arm around her waist.

As he helped her, the growing crowd that had

gathered at the sight of rescue began to disperse now the drama was over. Sarah stood at the shoreline shaking her head.

'That looked like some dip,' she said as Laura neared, eyeing up her handsome saviour.

Don't start, Laura warned her with her eyes. 'Yes, and thank you *so much* for helping. I probably wouldn't have survived had you not stood there and watched, you're a true hero,' Laura said to Sarah, her voice raspy from the salt water and thick with sarcasm. Sarah remained silent, she knew Laura made a good point.

'Will you be alright?' he said helping her sit down.

'She'll be fine,' Sarah said going to Laura's side. 'I think you should let us buy you a drink though.'

He looked at Laura, concern still etched on his face.

'If you're up to it?' he said.

'Of course she is,' Sarah said, digging her in the ribs, 'aren't you Laura?'

Laura nodded dumbfounded, still recovering from the incident.

'I'm David by the way.'

David and Laura had married one year to the day of their fateful meeting and not soon after, she had found out she was pregnant with their first child, James. David had been ecstatic – he was an attentive husband, lover and father. Laura dropped out of University to be a full time mother. She could not have been happier.

3

Why do I exist? Laura wondered to herself idly whilst sorting out the pile of clothes that needed ironing. As if in a trance, she picked out a shirt and laid it on its back, pressed the steam button, then ran the iron over the collar, slowly pressing it from one point to the other. She flipped the collar over to the other side to repeat the process. *Such an easy question, but profoundly difficult to answer*, she mused.

'Mummm, James is teasing me!' The loud, high-pitched voice snapped Laura out of her thoughts, abruptly bringing her back to reality.

'James, stop annoying your sister,' Laura said sternly for what seemed the hundredth time that week. The summer holidays had been a washout, which meant James and Emily had been confined to the house for most of it. They were both studious children who enjoyed mental stimulation; but they also had a never-ending energy supply that needed an outlet. Living in a coastal town with an outdated reputation as a retirement community such as Bournemouth, meant most of the activities the children took part in involved being outside or at its award-winning beaches. There'd been a promise of a "BBQ Summer", but as seemed the case every year, it had failed to materialise.

'I'm bored, why can't we go rock climbing now?' James whined as he popped his mop of blond hair around the door. At ten years old, he was already a heart-stopper with a smile that could charm you in a moment. *He's bored*, Laura thought, distastefully eyeing the mountain of clothes that still needed ironing. *You don't know what boredom is!* She felt like saying. Instead, she switched off the iron, relieved to have an excuse to stop for the day.

'Alright, alright, I will leave this until later. Do you want to ask Daniel and Ethan to join you? And I'll make supper for you all when we get back.'

'Cool,' he said, and in a flash he was gone and thundering up the stairs.

'What about me?' Emily whined, making her way down the hallway and into the utility room. 'Why do we always have to do the things he likes – it's not fair!' Laura laughed.

'You have the hearing of an owl,' she said, taking Emily's hand and lowering her tall, slender body until she was at her daughter's level. Both of them had emerald green eyes – Laura's full of light and laughter, Emily's brimming with tears.

'I thought you and I could go to the cinema tonight and watch *The Smurfs*,' she said, stroking her hair softly. 'How does that sound?'

'Can I invite Louise?' Emily asked eagerly, instantly forgetting all about James and her notion that he was favoured more because he was the eldest.

'Of course you can, darling.' She stood up and watched Emily's slim frame with long, silky, sandy hair skip happily out of the room, back to her normal lively and gregarious self.

Laura loosened her thick, golden-brown hair from her silver hairclip and ran her fingers through it with a sigh of relief. She didn't have to change out of her pale, faded jeans that fitted as if they had been made especially for her. Not only did they look good, but they were as comfortable as the white shirt that hugged her upper body. She opted for a pair of black, flat-heeled boots – the kind of footwear she generally preferred. Being five feet eight inches tall meant heels were unnecessary but on the few occasions when she did wear them, David still towered over her at six foot four.

Laura stood at the bottom of the oak staircase that led up to the four bedrooms and family bathroom.

'Come on, slow coaches, I thought you would have been ready by now.' At this, James ran down the stairs like a ball of energy, still tucking his t-shirt into his jeans. Emily was behind him, walking daintily like a little lady. Laura smiled – her daughter looked angelic dressed in her favourite white dress. Laura had been aghast when stores started selling thongs for young girls and t-shirts with suggestive slogans on them and was relieved that Emily still favoured more traditional clothing. 'Well don't you look the picture of perfection, Missy,' she said, kissing the top of her head when she reached the bottom step. Emily smiled, pleased that her choice of dress had the desired effect. Unlike her brother, she took pride in her appearance.

'Why, thank-you, Madame,' she said, giving her mother a twirl like she'd seen women do in the black and white films they watched together sometimes.

'Slow down before you hurt yourself!' Laura yelled as James rushed past her nearly knocking over the vase on the hall table but he took no notice as he continued to search for his trainers, rummaging through cupboards and moving furniture.

'In the living room.' Laura's annoyance was betrayed by her tone.

'Of course,' he said, playfully slapping himself on the side of the head. He sauntered to the living room, whistling to himself, a habit he'd picked up from his father.

'Come on then,' he said feigning impatience, 'we haven't got all day!' He walked to the large oak front door and pulled it ajar. A small dark figure shot through the gap as it opened. Ninja darted straight into the kitchen. It was his speed and stealth that made his name a natural choice. Many times, he had given Laura the fright of her life when he mysteriously appeared beside her without warning. Ninja's favourite pastime was ambushing David on the way back from the bathroom in the middle of the night. David was convinced the cat was trying to kill him.

'You two go and wait in the car whilst I feed Ninja,' she said as she fumbled through her bag looking for her car keys. Discovering them underneath her purse, she threw them to James.

'And James,' she called after him before he could jump down the four steps to the driveway, 'don't put the key in the ignition!'

He looked crestfallen, as Laura watched him unlock the car and slump into the passenger seat. She was always one-step ahead of him.

***

The drive to the sports centre was uneventful. James and Emily bickered over nothing as usual until Laura picked up Ethan and Daniel and James's attention switched to talking boy's stuff with his friends.

'The new *Assassin's Creed* game is awesome,' raged Daniel enthusiastically.

'Yeah, I've nearly finished it,' Ethan piped in with as much fervour as Daniel. When they stopped at a set of traffic lights, Emily looked up at her mother and rolled her eyes.

'Boys,' she said disinterestedly and turned back to look out of the window. Laura suppressed a smile. *Let's hope your attitude stays like that until you're at least sixty*, she thought to herself, *even if it is wishful thinking*.

It was just after midday when Laura manoeuvred her black Golf VW into the last parking space at the sports centre cark park. With school broken up for the summer holidays, she wasn't surprised that it was near capacity. It seemed everyone had the same idea of where to bring the kids on a rainy day.

Before she had even switched the ignition off, the boys had disengaged their seat belts, scrambled out of the vehicle and were racing towards the centre.

'I'll beat you to the door,' James shouted to the two boys lagging behind him.

Stepping out of the car, Laura inhaled deeply. The gentle breeze brought with it the fragrance of freshly cut grass. She could hear the echoes of her and her father laughing as the wet grass stained her feet green as she played barefoot in their garden. She smiled faintly as she surveyed the Dorset landscape, dotted with farms, hay bales and cows. It portrayed the unreal beauty of the picture postcards sold in tourist shops and she'd been surprised that planning permission had been granted to build the sports centre in such a prime location. She turned to watch Daniel and Ethan finally catch up with James at the entrance. The doors automatically slid open, letting out a blast of energy-pumping music, shattering the serenity of the countryside. As the boys disappeared inside, the doors slid closed and it was quiet again.

'Come on then,' she said to Emily, 'let's grab a snack while your brother pretends he's Tom Cruise.' Emily took her mother's hand and they walked towards the building. Just before they reached the doors, Laura heard her name being called.

'Laura, is that you?'

She spun around to see a woman with long brunette hair swept back away from her face, highlighting her natural beauty: clear hazel eyes lay behind long thick lashes, high cheekbones with a

smudge of blusher, and crimson plump lips. Laura
didn't recognise her at first, but slowly the realisation
dawned on her. It was her former best friend, Sarah. She
hadn't spoken to or seen her for two years now. Sarah
looked radiant – a vast improvement since they'd parted
ways. For a brief moment, they stood staring at each
other, neither knowing what to say. Sarah opened her
mouth to speak but Laura spoke first.

'Oh my god, Sarah,' she said faintly, unsure of
herself. She covered her mouth with her hand. 'What
are you doing here?'

'I didn't think much of the weather for a day at the
beach,' she said with a smile.

'You know what I mean! Here, in Bournemouth?'

Sarah shrugged.

'I'd had enough of London... There's only so much
pollution a girl can inhale!' she exclaimed, her face
shining. Laura moved quickly and embraced her friend
tightly as she felt tears welling up in her eyes.

'It's been so long,' she whispered, holding her
close.

'It feels like yesterday,' Sarah replied, holding her
tightly.

A tall, slender woman dressed smartly in a black,
belted Mac coat stood quietly in the background,
holding the hand of a girl the same height as Emily.
When Laura's attention finally turned to them, she
looked at the girl in disbelief. Sarah's daughter had
changed so much.

'Holly!' Laura said, enveloping her in an
affectionate hug. 'You must have grown at least two
inches.'

Holly smiled shyly.

'Laura...' Sarah said, bringing her attention to the
woman standing next to Holly, 'meet my friend Jada,

she has moved to back to Bournemouth with me.' Laura reached out to shake Jada's slender hand.

'I've heard so much about you,' Jada said, her wide friendly smile revealing a perfect set of white teeth, her light hazel eyes radiating warmth. Her olive-skinned complexion was framed by a mass of unruly dark brown curls.

'I can only imagine,' Laura said, smiling back at the stunning woman in front of her. Emily stood stiffly as Sarah approached her.

'Hello Emily,' she said apprehensively. 'It's lovely to see you... I haven't seen you for such a long time.'

'No, you haven't,' she said, hostility in her voice. She was still angry at the way Sarah had just disappeared with Holly out of the blue – she hadn't even had a chance to say goodbye to her best friend, who she'd looked upon as a sister. Holly approached her mother and Emily.

'Hello Emily,' Holly said awkwardly.

'You've grown,' was all Emily could think of to say.

'So have you,' Holly replied. Her dark brown hair was bunched into two ponytails, giving her a much younger appearance than her eight years.

'I like your outfit,' Emily said, referring to Holly's black, embellished jogging suit. 'James is inside – shall we go and find him? He won't believe it when he sees you,' she continued excitedly. Holly turned to her mum.

'Is it okay if we go inside?'

'Yes, we'll be right behind you,' Sarah said as she took ten pounds out of her pocket. 'Go and get yourselves something to drink,' she said, handing the money to Holly.

'Thanks, Mum,' Holly said and grabbed the note. Both girls ran off towards the centre holding hands.

Laura had seen the cool reception Emily had given Sarah and stepped towards her, putting a comforting hand on her shoulder.

'I'm sorry,' Laura said, seeing the hurt in Sarah's eyes.

'No, I'm the one that's sorry – Emily has every right to be angry with me,' she paused. 'And so do you.' Her face was full of remorse.

'You had your reasons,' Laura replied sympathetically. 'I don't know what I would have done if I were in your shoes.' Pain flickered across the women's eyes. 'Anyway, how have you been?' Sarah said, consciously changing the subject.

'Everything's great, and you look amazing,' she smiled, admiring the way the denim skinny jeans, vintage denim jacket and white ruffled top she wore looked on her.

'Thanks, I feel great too,' Sarah replied enthusiastically.

'Why didn't you let me know you were back?' Laura asked.

'I was going to call you when I settled in.' Over the last two years, she had toyed with the idea of getting in touch with Laura several times, but in the end, she had decided not to. She didn't know if Laura could forgive her for the way she had treated her.

'Are you back for good? Laura asked, unsure if she was ready for the answer.

'Yes, I've come back Laura... For good,' she added when she saw a flicker of doubt pass over Laura's face.

'I'm so glad,' she said touching the side of Sarah's face. 'I really am... Does Joe know you're back?' she asked.

'No, and I don't think he'd care if he knew we were,' Sarah replied tersely, her demeanour changing at the sound of Joe's name. Above, the clouds towed dark shadows, threatening rain. Sarah looked up and then motioned towards the door. 'Let's go inside and you can tell me what I've been missing for the past two years.' She took Laura and Jada by the arm and led both women into the complex just as the first drops of rain fell from the sky.

***

Laura arrived home to the sound of the phone ringing. She ran to answer it, still a little shocked about her encounter an hour previously.

'I'm going to be home late tonight,' David said.

'Again?' Laura asked, kicking off her shoes as James and Emily sprinted upstairs to their bedrooms.

''Fraid so. Kiss the kids for me?'

'Ok, but before you go, guess who I bumped into today?' she asked.

'I have no idea... shock me.'

'Sarah!' she said dramatically.

'Really, my god, how is she?'

'She looks amazing, she's doing really well, and Holly has grown so much,' Laura said enthusiastically.

'It'll be good to see them again...'

'She's in Bournemouth with a friend of hers from London,' Sarah said, filling him in on her earlier conversation with Sarah. 'She said Joe hasn't seen Holly in an age... It just goes to show, you never really know anybody, do you. I thought he would be the last person on this earth to have no contact with his daughter.'

'... Anyway,' David interrupted, wanting to steer the conversation in another direction. 'When are you going to see Sarah again?' Joe was still a touchy subject. Although they were still business partners,

Laura rarely saw him except on the odd occasion when she accompanied David to a work meal.

'I've invited Sarah and her friend over for dinner at the weekend. Emily is so excited, Holly is going to be staying overnight and - '

'Listen, I've got to run, I'm due in court, don't wait up,' David cut in before she could finish.

'Ok, love you,' she said, smiling into the phone.

There was no reply from the other end. He had already hung up.

It was after midnight when Laura heard the front door slam shut and loud footsteps making their way up the staircase and into their bedroom. He tried to undress in the dark, making a bad job of it – he'd obviously had one too many vodkas.

'Put the light on before you hurt yourself,' Laura said sleepily.

'Did I wake you?' David slurred, fumbling for the switch.

'No, not at all,' she lied, moving her arm across her face to cover her eyes from the glare of the light.

'Are the kids alright?'

'Yes, they're fine. Ethan and Daniel came over for dinner so I ended up taking them all to the cinema.' Laura sat up, suddenly feeling more awake.

'Sounds like fun,' he said, eventually removing his shirt.

'Do you fancy some adult fun?' she asked, casting an admiring look over his bare chest. He had it all going for him: slim waist, well-defined muscles, a handsome face and devastating smile. He rubbed his well-toned stomach.

'As tempting as it sounds, I don't think I'd last a minute,' he said as he switched off the light and collapsed onto the bed.

She flopped back down, disappointed. In the past few months, something had changed. The late nights, the lack of sexual intimacy. She couldn't bring herself to believe that David might be having an affair – he barely had the chance to sit down, his schedule was so busy. The fact he had lost weight since starting the manslaughter case convinced her it was no more than burnout.

'I love you,' she whispered in his ear. He groaned a response and fell asleep, leaving her awake. She loved him so much; she didn't know what she would possibly do without him.

4

'Have I told you how lucky I am to have you in my life?' Sarah slurred.

'Yes, many times.' Laura smiled fondly at her.

'Who would have thought that I would end up marrying David's colleague and we'd both be pregnant at the same time? We have got to be the luckiest women alive, do you know that, to actually find real love and all of this,' she said, waving her arms around the generously proportioned dining room. She brought the wine glass to her mouth and took a deep gulp.

'Oh, I'm sure you could think of something to add to everything else you've already got,' her husband said, returning from having a cigarette in the garden and slumping down on a chair at the table.

'No – you're wrong Joe,' she said as she turned to him. 'I have you, who I love very much, and we have our friends – how many people are lucky enough to have friends like Laura and Dave?' She raised her glass up in the air unsteadily.

'I'll drink to that,' David said, reaching across the table and clinking her glass.

'I wish I could just freeze this moment in time where everything is so perfect,' she said, sadly.

'Will you be thinking everything is perfect in the morning?' Joe asked, an almost swooning sense of revolution sweeping over him. It was a scene that had been well played out before. The two couples met every other weekend for drinks and dinner and inevitably, once the alcohol was flowing Sarah's personality totally changed. Her drunken blathering normally continued nonstop.

'Yes I will tomorrow, and the day after, and the day after that, blah-de-blah-de-blah.' Her voice trailed off as she took her husband's face in her hands and pulled it towards hers. 'You are so yummy I could eat you,' she said, planting a kiss on his mouth.

'Easy,' he said with a humourless smile, easing her back into her chair. He reached over for the wine bottle and poured a generous amount of the red liquid into each of the three glasses, deliberately ignoring Sarah's one.

'So guys, have we decided where we're going for the school holidays next month? We had better book soon otherwise we may end up camping again,' Laura reminded them, laughing. They all groaned, only partly in jest as they recalled the disastrous camping trip they had taken when everywhere else they had tried to book for the Easter holidays the year before had been sold out. They had ended up spending a week in a muddy field trying to keep three bored kids entertained.

'We could always hire a villa in the south of France,' David suggested.

'Yes, we could go over by Eurostar,' Laura added, excited at the thought.

'As long as there's booze, I'm in!' Sarah said taking another gulp of wine and spilling some of it on her blouse.

'Yeah, that's about right isn't it,' Joe remarked irritably. Though Sarah was drunk, she did not miss the tone in Joe's voice.

'And what the fuck is that supposed to mean?' she asked him, putting the glass unsteadily on the table.

'Do you really need to ask?' he flared back at her, taking a cigarette out of his shirt pocket and lighting it. He took a deep drag. Sarah tried to grab the cigarette out of his mouth.

'I thought you said there was no smoking in the house,' she spat, grabbing for his cigarette again. He moved the chair back so she could not reach him.

'Well it's my fucking house and I will do what the fuck I want in it. I'm the one that fucking slaves away a hundred hours a week so you can sit there and tell everyone what a fucking great life you have.' The liberating effects of the alcohol had put him in a fighting mood.

'Come on Joe, this isn't necessary,' David said interrupting.

'Isn't it?' he snarled, 'Are you going to tell me what I can and can't do in my own fucking house as well?' he asked aggressively. Nobody spoke for several seconds. Laura looked over at Sarah and her heart bled for her. She looked so young and vulnerable. She went over to her and helped her stand, then glanced at Joe and said, 'I fancy one of those cigarettes, do you mind?'

He gave her a tight smile, grateful that she had diffused the situation. She felt a melting of his brief hostility as he lit her fresh cigarette and handed it to her.

'Come on Sarah, let's go and pretend we're having a sneaky fag behind the bike shed,' she said guiding her towards the patio doors that led into the garden. Sarah still had not spoken. She followed Laura in a daze. As she passed Joe, she put her hand gently on his shoulder.

'I'm sorry,' she said meekly.

'I'm the one that's sorry,' he said without looking up at her.

***

That night Laura had difficulty sleeping. She felt uneasy about what had happened between Sarah and Joe. This was not the first time that she had seen them argue but something about Joe's demeanour that evening had been different. David had fallen fast asleep when they got home and whilst she felt bad for doing it she nudged him several times until he woke.

'What did Joe say to you when we were in the garden?' she asked him. He groaned something and tried to go back to sleep. 'Please David, this is important, what did he say?' she kept on at him, shaking his shoulder. He let out a big sigh.

'Just that he didn't think there was going to be a group holiday next month.'

'Did he say why?' she asked, leaning closer to him.

'Not really,' he said sleepily.

'What do you mean, "not really"? Either he said something or he didn't. Which is it?' His evasiveness was beginning to irritate her.

'Do we really have to do this right now, for god's sake? I'm bloody tired,' he groaned, covering his head with the pillow.

'If you think that attitude is going to get me off your back you're mistaken. Just tell me what he said and I'll leave you alone.' Defeated, he removed the pillow and rubbed his hand over his face, sighing.

'He said they're having big problems at the moment.'

'Like what?' she asked. Sarah hadn't said anything to her, and if there had been any problems, she was the first who'd have heard about it. 'Does Sarah know about these problems?'

'Look, you were in the garden for what, five minutes; we didn't exactly have time for an "Oprah" moment. That's all he said and I didn't push it, now for Pete's sake, can I go to sleep?'

'Okay.' She kissed him on the forehead and lay back down.

'Darling,' he said sweetly.

'Yes?' she asked, knowing that tone of voice.

'Any chance you can get me a glass of water please?'

'Oooh, the cheek of you,' she said, getting out of bed. She was halfway down the hall when he called out, 'Watch out for Ninja... ' but his warning was too late – she'd already screamed. He hid his face in the pillow to muffle his laughter.

***

The impending calamity, which had been lurking in the shadows, happened suddenly and without warning. Barely a week had passed when a panic-stricken Laura burst in on David whilst he was having a bath.

'What's the matter?' He immediately became alert. 'Are the kids alright?' he asked, getting out of the bath and quickly putting on his robe.

'Yes, they're fine,' she said with urgency in her voice. 'It's Sarah – I have to go there, something is wrong,' she said, trying to catch her breath. 'Just watch the kids and tell Holly she'll be staying here tonight. I'll let you know what's happening as soon as I can.'

'Shall I call my Mum and get her to come and watch them? I can come with you,' he asked, worried about Laura going over there by herself.

'Yes, okay, but meet me there after she arrives – I have to go,' she said as she ran down the stairs and out the front door.

Fifteen minutes later, she was on Sarah's doorstep, banging on the door, trying to be heard over the sounds of screaming coming from inside.

'Please don't leave me, please,' she heard her begging pathetically. 'Joe, I'm sorry; I'll do whatever you want but please don't leave me... please...'

Laura kept banging until Sarah opened the door –

her tear-streaked face was blotchy, her hair wild. She fell into Laura's extended arms, her body racked with sobs.

'He's leaving me, Laura,' she said, releasing herself from the embrace to look up at Laura, her eyes like those of a wounded animal.

'Please tell him not to leave me, please, I'll do anything,' Sarah cried.

'Let's go inside,' Laura said, turning Sarah around and leading her through the front door. 'Where's Joe?' Sarah pointed up the stairs.

'In our bedroom,' she said meekly.

'You wait down here,' Laura said as though talking to a child. 'David will be here shortly. I'll talk to Joe in the meantime. Will you be alright for a minute?' Sarah nodded her head dumbly.

Taking two steps at a time, Laura reached the landing and stopped for a moment to catch her breath. As she entered the master bedroom she found Joe with his back to the door, a large suitcase laid out on the bed in front of him. Several piles of clothes were strewn across it. He leant forward, picking up each item of clothing then quickly throwing it into the case.

'Joe?' Laura called him softly. He turned to look at her slowly.

'Don't waste your time, Laura, I'm leaving this time and nothing is going to stop me,' he said bluntly.

This time Laura thought. *Had there been other times that Sarah hadn't told her about?*

'Joe, if you feel anything for Sarah and Holly you cannot walk out of here and leave her in this state,' she said, trying to make him see reason. 'Please Joe, if not for Sarah, then for Holly.'

They could both hear the low whimpers from Sarah at the bottom of the stairs. Laura walked over to

Joe, tears flowing freely from her eyes.

'Joe, you can work this out. You can't turn your back on your marriage just like that.'

He stopped packing, slumped onto the bed and rested his face in his hands. She knelt down in front of him. 'Listen to me Joe – you're going to need to call the doctor, okay? She's in a bad way. Promise me you won't leave tonight so I can help my friend - your wife. Promise me, Joe,' she pleaded.

'I can't Laura, I'm sorry, I really am,' he said. 'Go and look after her, she's going to need you. I'll call the doctor.'

He stood up, took his mobile phone from his pocket and pressed a button. As he began speaking to the doctor, Laura left the room feeling defeated. Could this really be happening to her closest, dearest friends? She walked slowly down the stairs, one-step at a time, dreading reaching the bottom and having to tell Sarah that she had been unable to change Joe's mind. She sighed deeply as she reached the bottom step where Sarah was hunched over in a ball.

'Come on,' Laura said, trying to coax Sarah from the stairs. She took her arm and heaved her up. 'David will talk some sense into him when he arrives,' she said, a little too optimistically. Sarah was reluctantly led into the living room where she immediately threw herself onto the large sofa and wept with fury, indignation, desolation and sorrow. Laura sat down beside her and gently stroked her back. The right words to say eluded her.

The tall, long-nosed doctor arrived carrying a battered black case and with an anxious look on his face. After thanking him profusely for arriving so soon, Laura led him into the living room and closed the door gently behind him, leaving them alone to speak privately. She paced up and down the passage, anxiously wishing David would hurry and take control of the situation. He was good with things like this. His calm nature in any given drama was what made him such a great solicitor.

She stopped and peered closely at the photographs adorning the walls, all displaying the image of a perfect family. Joe, Sarah and Holly, smiling at the camera, not a care in the world. Parts of their lives captured in a split second. Laura turned away when she heard the living room door open. The doctor exited the room, a grim look on his face as Laura approached him.

'How is she?' she asked, concern etched on her face.

'I've given Sarah a sedative for now, it should get her through the night,' he said kindly. 'I suggest bringing her by the surgery tomorrow if this situation doesn't sort itself out tonight.' Laura nodded her head, sadness in her eyes. As they reached the door, the doorbell rang.

'That will be my husband,' she explained to the doctor for no apparent reason. She let the doctor out and her husband in. 'What's going on?' he said in a whispered voice glancing around the hallway. Laura motioned for David to go to the living room where Sarah lay on the sofa in a deep sleep. She put her finger to her lips instructing him not to speak and gently pulled him away from the door entrance.

'Joe is upstairs. Please go and make him see some sense,' she said gently steering him to the staircase. 'I'll sit with Sarah,' she continued, more to herself than David.

As she heard him walk up the stairs and reach the landing, she went back into the living room and sat opposite her sleeping friend. Sarah looked so vulnerable. She stared at her for a long time, trying to understand the transformation she had seen take place this evening, with this woman who was so confident in every aspect of her life, who didn't take crap from anybody. Independent Sarah – she thought she knew her, but she was slowly realising that she didn't really know her at all.

David and Joe sat quietly for a long time in silence. David knew that when Joe was ready to speak he would, and he knew better than to push him.

'I've got a problem, Dave,' he said eventually. David leaned forward.

'What problem?' he asked, perplexed. Joe looked down.

'I can't help but want to sleep with every woman I see. I've never been faithful to Sarah, I'm just not a one woman man,' he said after a few moments.

'What do you mean?' David said. He was well aware of what Joe was saying but he wanted to buy himself some time to deal with the shock of what he'd just heard.

'I've met someone who I'm going to move in with for a while, Dave,' he said. 'I'm sick of all this bullshit. I'm sick of being led about like a dog on a lead. Being told what I can and can't do, who I can see, what I should wear, how much I can drink, how much time I should be spending with Holly.' He paused, his eyes glassy. 'What about me, Dave?' he asked. 'Where do my wants and needs fit into all this? This is my life, but it feels like someone else's.' He paused briefly, somewhat embarrassed. 'For Christ sake I'm starting to sound like a bloody woman!'

'Who is she?' David asked, not sure he wanted to hear the answer.

'It doesn't matter who she is, what matters is that

she's shaken me out of this dream world I was sleep-walking in. You do know I only married Sarah because she was pregnant?' he said regretfully. David shook his head in astonishment.

'Yep. I fell into that trap because I couldn't keep my dick in my pants.'

'Why didn't you tell me?' Joe shrugged.

'It's not something I'm proud of you know, that I threw my life away because of a shag.'

'You didn't have to marry her! Jesus, we aren't in the bloody nineteenth century – she could have had an abortion or you could have made an arrangement of some kind,' David said, starting to lose his cool.

'I know, I know,' Joe said, exasperated. He got up and walked to the window. 'I thought maybe settling down would be better than being single – you were married and had a kid, I guess I just felt I was being left behind.' He stared out of the window, contemplating his life.

'I never had you down as being one of the sheep; I looked up to you because you weren't a follower like me. I thought you really loved Sarah and was happy you were going to be a dad.'

Joe turned around and glanced at David, unable to look him in the eye. 'You know me Dave, I always roll with the punches,' he laughed bitterly. 'With the amount of emotional blackmail she loaded on my back I'm surprised I even managed to walk down the aisle with the weight of it.'

'So who's the girl you've met now then?' David asked again, bracing himself.

'If I tell you, I don't want to hear any judgemental bullshit, because you don't know her,' he said defensively as he paced the room.

'Calm down Joe, bloody hell, the way you're carrying

on it's as if she's from another planet!'

'She might as well be.'

David looked confused. 'Why, what's wrong with her?' he asked.

'She's on the game,' he said, with not a hint of embarrassment.

David stood up. 'What!' he shouted, his face turning crimson.

'Shhhh!' Joe said quickly, putting his finger to his mouth.

'Oh, don't worry about your wife hearing anything,' David said sarcastically. 'She's just been knocked out by the doctor because her dick of a husband is leaving her and his daughter for a whore. Jesus Christ, this just gets worse.'

'I told you there wasn't any point telling you, I knew you wouldn't understand.' Joe pouted like a child.

'That's the only thing you've been right about.' He sat back down and put his head in his hands. 'Joe, what are you doing?'

'I'm doing what's right for me, Dave, and the least you can do is spare a thought for me and what I want. Sarah and Holly will want for nothing, you know that. I just can't live like this anymore.'

'Dare I ask how long has this been going on? And please tell me you've been using protection!'

'Of course I used protection, I'm not that stupid!'

David raised his eyebrows but remained silent.

'A few weeks,' Joe said sheepishly.

'A few weeks!' David yelled in disbelief. 'Let me get this straight – you are throwing your marriage...' Joe interrupted him. 'It's not a marriage, it never has been, so no, I'm not throwing anything away. I'm trying to be happy for once.'

'So how do you know that this girl is going to make you happy? The first whore you sleep with you fall in love with.'

'She wasn't the first Dave, there were plenty of others before her,' he confessed.

David's face paled. He couldn't believe what he was hearing.

'She isn't a big deal Dave, she just said I could stay there until I get myself sorted,' Joe said, resuming packing clothes into his case.

'Don't do this Joe,' David said, suddenly wary.

Joe turned to look at his friend. 'I can't believe this. After all I've told you, you still think the best thing for me to do would be to stay with a woman I don't love? Is that what you would really want for me, to grow into a middle-age sucker with a life full of regrets?'

'Of course not,' David said, his voice softening.

'Then be happy for me, I would be if the tables were turned.' He zipped up the case and with a heave dragged it onto the floor.

'I'm just worried Joe – what if you're making the biggest mistake of your life?'

'I already did that,' he said solemnly. He gave David a slap on the shoulder. 'When I get settled you and Laura can come round for a meal – she's a great cook,' he said beaming with the thought of his new life ahead of him.

When hell freezes over, David thought. The very idea that Laura, Sarah's best friend, would sit at the same table as *one* of the women who was responsible for the breakup of their marriage convinced David, more than ever, that Joe was not in his right mind.

When Joe quietly left the family home that night he told himself he wasn't being a coward by not facing his daughter and wife in the morning. He convinced himself that it would not be beneficial to anybody to have another scene like there had been earlier that evening. Besides, he couldn't wait to go to his new home and be with Crystal *all night.*

When Sarah awoke the next morning feeling as if she had been kicked in the head, the look on Laura's face answered her question. Joe had gone – and it would be a bitter pill for her to swallow. She had invested her whole future in him and now she was alone. She buried her head in the cushion and sobbed. For what was, and for what the future held for her and her daughter. She found a bottle of vodka in the kitchen and drank several mouthfuls one after the other, trying to numb the persistent pain.

'Sarah, that's not the answer,' Laura said, attempting to take the glass from her hand. Sarah stepped back, pushing her away. She stood leaning against the worktop looking at Laura through an alcoholic haze.

'Did you know?' Sarah asked accusingly.

'Of course I didn't know, how could you ask such a thing?' Laura said, hurt from the inference.

'Did David know?' she asked more aggressively.

'No,' Laura said, a little unsure.

'You're lying,' she said. 'You're fucking lying to me; you've all been lying to me.' Her eyes narrowed – all the anger she had bottled up inside her suddenly flowing freely. 'I'm the big joke, it seems.'

Laura tried to comfort her but she shook her off.

'Get out of my house,' she said, pushing Laura towards the front door. 'Get the fuck out of my house...' she screamed. Her face flushed furiously. Laura's attempts to diffuse her anger were futile.

'I don't want to see either of you again – do you hear me?' she said, giving Laura one final push through the front door and slamming it shut. 'I don't need friends like you,' she shouted, her voice quivering with anger. 'I don't need anybody.'

'Mum?' Surprised, she spun round to find her daughter cowering at the bottom of the stairs. David must have bought her home earlier that morning.

'Come here, baby,' Sarah said, grasping for her but falling on her knees.

'Mum, you're frightening me.' Tears welled in her eyes.

'It'll be alright, baby,' she slurred, 'I promise I'll make things alright.'

The following day, though her head ached and her heart was broken, she packed cases, made phone calls and walked out of the family home for the last time. She would take Holly to stay with her parents until she could find a more permanent base. She didn't want to see any of the people who claimed they loved her ever again.

5

'Sorry I'm late,' David said as he entered the dining room, interrupting the women's conversation. 'Had a meeting sprung on me at the last minute.' Sarah stood up to greet him and they embraced for a long time.

'It's good to see you David,' Sarah said, seemingly overwhelmed with emotion. He held her at arm's length.

'You look wonderful,' he remarked genuinely.

'You don't look too bad yourself,' she joked, regaining her composure.

'And you,' he said releasing Sarah and looking over her shoulder, 'must be Jada.' Jada smiled, arose from her chair and stretched out a slender hand.

'Nice to meet you, David.' He shook her hand gently then motioned towards the stairs.

'I'm just going to shower and change.' He bent down and kissed Laura on the head. 'Won't be a mo.'

He made his way upstairs listening to the raucous laughter from the three women as they continued their conversation. As he undressed, he inwardly winced as a sharp pain shot through his abdomen. He rubbed it gently until the pain subsided. Quickly showering and putting on a pair of jeans, shirt and loafers, he re-joined his wife and guests in the middle of a conversation about how Sarah and Jada had met.

'Well, funnily enough, we met on a cruise ship,' Sarah said, looking at Laura to gauge her reaction.

'Really?' Laura asked her surprise apparent.

'Yes, I know,' Sarah said bashfully, 'I wouldn't have believed it either, who would have thought I would have dragged my sorry arse onto a cruise ship for Christmas – alone... but it was one of the best things I ever did.'

'Not that we had much time to relax on board – if it wasn't Sarah getting hit on by randy old men, it was me. I think their poor wives were relieved they were being left alone!' Jada added. They all laughed.

'We're not talking about sixty year olds here either,' Sarah continued, 'they were at least seventy plus. I think an age limit should have been imposed on the distribution of Viagra. No one above forty-five should be allowed them!' she said with a wry smile.

'Ahh, that's not fair,' Laura laughed.

'Can you imagine how relieved the old dears were when their husbands reached sixty and couldn't get it up? The last thing they would have expected was for their todgers to be given a new lease of life! Men are undoubtedly thrilled to have their sexual potency restored, I'm sure but it's their poor wives I feel sorry for!' Sarah said, starting to feel the effects of her third large glass of wine.

'Well, I bet some women would be more than happy to be able to share a passionate night with their husband,' David interjected, feigning annoyance.

'Yes... for ten minutes perhaps, but two hours!' Jada laughed.

'Well, if he can't get his satisfaction at home he'll just look elsewhere for it,' David said with mock seriousness.

'Let's not even go down this road,' Laura said, wanting to kick David under the table and thinking of how many times Joe had been unfaithful to Sarah. She looked at Sarah but her face was neutral and David looked oblivious to the insensitive comment he had made.

'So how's business, Dave?' Sarah asked after several seconds of silence.

'Busy. I sometimes wonder what the hell we've let

ourselves in for,' he said, fiddling with his wine glass.

'I bet Joe's loving the workload, he always was a workaholic.'

'He's not human that bloke,' David laughed, 'he's first in and last out, I don't know how he does it.'

'Things haven't changed there, then,' she said. 'And how is he doing?' Sarah enquired curiously.

'He's doing fine,' David said sheepishly, looking at Laura for a cue to see how much he should say.

'I'm happy for him,' Sarah said without the slightest hint of animosity. 'Life's too short to be miserable. I learnt that the hard way. You've got to take happiness where you can find it – it's a rarity when you do,' she said.

A look passed between David and Sarah and was gone in a flash. Laura thought perhaps she'd imagined it. Shaking her head, she said

'I'm going to plate up dinner. David can you refresh everyone's glasses please?'

'With pleasure,' he said, opening a bottle of red wine as Laura left the room. 'I'm glad to see you haven't turned into a tee-total bore. Have you noticed that when people near their thirties their alcohol consumption drops?' he said with a humorous smile.

'Not really. Not me, anyway,' Sarah laughed.

'Good, so let lets drink and be merry,' he said holding his glass up to the women as Laura walked in with two plates of mouth-watering food consisting of slow-roasted Tuscan pork with roast garlic mash and al dente broccoli as a side dish. The aromas were a banquet.

'I've told the kids they can eat on their laps,' Laura said as she placed a plate in front of both of her guests, 'they're just about to start watching the new Torn movie.'

'Wow, this tastes amazing!' Jada said enthusiastically after her first mouthful.

'Thank you,' Laura said humbly as she forked the food on her plate, 'I've always found it tastes more like lamb then pork.'

'David,' Sarah said between mouthfuls of food, 'not to put you on the spot but can you let Joe know I'll be coming in to see him on Monday? I think it's time we spoke about his plans for Holly.'

'Of course I will,' he said.

'Thanks, Holly pretends she doesn't care about seeing him but I know she hurts like hell. All this change hasn't been easy for her.'

'I can imagine,' Laura said, shaking her head.

'Looking back now I know we should never have gotten married but we were young and naive,' she said looking wistful. 'I blamed myself for a long time, but I've come to the realisation that it wasn't anybody's fault, our relationship was simply built on the wrong type of foundation.' She shrugged. 'I was superficial, I guess. I still needed to find myself, and Joe, well he just wanted to get his leg over! Perfect match, or so I thought. Who knows what would have happened had I not gotten pregnant – I think he would have tired of me eventually.' She shrugged again. 'Who knows.'

***

Sarah opened the door to the contemporary three-bedroom apartment and walked straight into the luxury kitchen, leaving Jada in the hallway as she removed her coat.

'Tea, or something stronger?' she called out to Jada.

'What are you having?'

'I think I'll have a glass of wine,' she said as she

opened the wine cooler and removed a bottle.

'Wine it is then,' Jada said, retrieving two glasses from the cupboard and placing them on the worktop.

Glasses in hand, they made their way into the living room and sat on the sofa in front of the large, seamless, tinted glass windows, admiring the panoramic views which spread right across the ocean from Hengistbury Head and the Isle of Wight in the east, to the Isle of Purbeck in the west.

'Are you glad you came back?' Jada asked Sarah finally.

'Yes, I just wish it had been under happier circumstances,' she said with a tinge of sadness.

'I know.'

'Did you enjoy yourself?' Sarah asked, sipping her wine, enjoying the crispness of it.

'Very much so, in fact I'm really looking to seeing them again. I really enjoyed their company.'

'I'm glad – they really are a great couple.'

Jada leant forward and kissed Sarah full on the lips, parting them with her tongue. The sweetness of Jada's tongue sent a throbbing sensation through her body. She was still amazed at this potential for heat and passion.

'Is it wrong for me to feel randy under these circumstances?' Sarah asked, arching her eyebrow, a trace of guilt on her face.

'No,' Jada said, losing herself in Sarah's eyes. 'Not at all.' She slowly unbuttoned Sarah's blouse, looking hungrily at her hardened nipples hidden beneath a red lace bra, her taut stomach contracting as Jada suggestively ran the tip of her finger over it, teasing her with how low she would go. Sarah eloquently removed her blouse and unhooked her bra, revealing her firm breasts. She shook her brunette, silky hair loose, the fragrance of shampoo and perfume filling the air. She smiled seductively at Jada.

'Do you like what you see?' she asked, her voice husky with emotion.

'Always,' Jada whispered.

Sarah still felt butterflies every time she looked at her lover's body. She loved touching her, feeling the softness of her skin, the feminine smell of her scent. Jada bent over and without touching her, teasingly circled her nipple with the tip of her tongue. Sarah released a quick breath. She cupped Jada's face and brought it level to hers. They gazed into each other's eyes, heat smouldering between them and their lips met again. Jada's hand slid over Sarah's breasts as she kissed her deeply and passionately. She pushed Sarah down on her back, quickly removing her own top and bra before lying at her side, savouring the warm naked skin against her own. Caressing her neck with her lips, she slowly slid her hand up Sarah's skirt. With mounting excitement Sarah breathed hard, quivering in anticipation as she felt her underwear being pushed aside and Jada's fingers probing her womanhood. She let out a little cry of delight as Jada's hand increased the pressure and moved faster in and out of her being. Sarah's breathing was ragged as she became ready to climax when Jada suddenly withdrew her hand. Sarah looked at her with disappointment, her upper lip warm with perspiration.

'Don't look so sad,' Jada laughed, 'you'll be having plenty of what you want – we have the whole night...' She stood up from the sofa, took Sarah's hand in hers, and led her through to their bedroom.

6

The saying that "love always hits you when you least expect it" had certainly been true for Sarah and Jada. Reeling from a bitter divorce and needing a break, Sarah had decided to take a much-deserved holiday for the festive season. Holly wanted to spend Christmas with her Grandfather so Sarah had the perfect opportunity to get away from it all. She'd received a generous settlement from her divorce and the sale of their house, and with a click of the mouse, she had impulsively booked a ten-day cruise around the Canary Islands.

A week later, she was boarding the enormous ship in Southampton, wondering if she had made the right decision. *Ten days is a long time to be alone*, she thought to herself as she looked at the families and lovers boarding ahead of her. She'd never considered taking a cruise before that day; the thought of being stuck on a floating hotel with hundreds of strangers had never appealed to her, but now she looked forward to the anonymity it would bring. Nobody knew her, knew that she was divorced or that her bastard of an ex-husband had been cheating on her at every opportunity.

As the floating hotel made its way out of the harbour, Sarah stood at the rail and whatever doubts she'd had about taking a cruise dissipated as she gazed out into the never-ending horizon in front of her. Christmas carols played on the speakers and feelings of apprehension were replaced with a girlish, tingly feeling as she felt herself switch into a holiday mood.

A small, pot-bellied porter with grey hair shaven closely to his head advised her that her cabin was ready. She thanked him and handed him a five-pound tip.

'If there is anything else I can help you with please

let me know Madam,' he said, handing her the cabin's key.

Bloody hell, she thought, *I'm being called Madam now – I must be getting old!* She pushed open the small door and was pleased with what she saw. The suite was exactly as it had looked on the Internet. It was luxurious, but not to the point of being distasteful. The space had been used effectively – there was an open plan living room and bedroom plus plenty of storage for the mountain of clothes Sarah had brought with her. The large white tiles and light blue border in the bathroom gave it a spacious feel and outside the large window was a small balcony, large enough to house two deck chairs, a table and two chairs.

She eyed it approvingly as she thought about having breakfast out there with the sun and sound of the sea being her only companions. Chilled champagne stood in a silver ice bucket with two fine crystal glasses set beside it. She removed one of the glasses from the tray and with an expert hand, she popped the champagne cork, tilted the glass to the side and slowly filled the glass, watching the bubbles explode as they made their way through the neck of the bottle.

'To me,' she said to her reflection in the mirror as she lifted the glass to her mouth. Placing the empty glass back on the tray, she picked up the itinerary from the table and rechecked the destinations: Funchal, Santa Cruz, San Sebastian, Las Palmas and Lisbon.

This is going to be a holiday to remember. Infused with a feeling of warmth, she poured herself another glass. *It feels great not having to answer to anybody,* she thought as she slipped her shoes off and lay on the sofa feeling pleased with herself.

Hours later and feeling peckish, Sarah dressed in a slick black number for dinner and headed for the restaurant but found herself seated with a flirtatious eighty-year-old man who engaged her in boring conversation for the duration of dinner. A woman sitting opposite her piqued her attention. Seemingly in a world of her own, she looked like she modelled for Vogue – her makeup had been applied artfully and her dark brown hair was pulled into a bun at the back of her head, highlighting her elegant bone structure. She was dressed in a stylish two-piece black suit which accentuated her figure. Sarah noticed that she picked at her food, not paying any attention to the middle-aged man sitting next to her and looking at them both as though they were part of the menu.

After what seemed an age, Sarah finally managed to disentangle herself from her boring dinner companion and headed for the deck to get some fresh air. She stood at the guardrail, looking up at the black ceiling of sky; thousands upon thousands of immortal stars dusting it. It was awe-inspiring – she felt small and insignificant.

'Lovely evening, isn't it?' a male voice said behind her. With a touch of irritation, she turned around to face him.

'Yes, it is,' she said, turning back to look at the stars. She hoped he would get the message and leave her alone but he chose not to take the hint and she could feel the intensity of his stare.

'Do you fancy a night cap?' he asked, suggestively stroking her bare arm. He was short and square jawed with dark eyes and neatly parted hair. He looked well groomed and was obviously wealthy, which accounted for his over confident attitude.

Oh god, this is just what I need, she thought despairingly. Thankfully, they were interrupted before she could reply.

'There you are! Sorry to have kept you waiting,

there was a queue in the ladies.' Sarah whirled round to see who her saviour was and was surprised to see the beautiful woman she'd been admiring earlier.

'That's okay,' Sarah said playing along, 'I was just about to tell...' she said, looking at the male intruder, fishing for his name.

'Gavin,' he said tightly.

'Gavin,' she continued, 'that I had plans for tonight – and every other night,' she said as she looped Jada's arm. 'Thanks anyway,' she said as they walked away, giggling.

'Thank you so much for that,' Sarah said as they made their way below deck.

'That's okay,' Jada replied, 'I saw the way he was looking at you over dinner – when you left and he left straight after I thought I'd just check and make sure you were safe.'

'Safe and sound thanks to you,' Sarah said gratefully. 'Well, this is me,' she said when they reached her cabin.

'Well I'm in cabin 10, so if creepy-balls shows his face, give me a call!' Sarah laughed.

'I will,' she said as she let herself in. She shut the door behind her but a second later she threw it open again and poked her head out, calling to Jada halfway down the corridor.

'Do you fancy breakfast tomorrow?' she called after her.

'Sure,' Jada said, and Sarah fell asleep that night feeling happier than she had in what felt like a very long time.

Breakfast was served on the outside deck.

'If you have no objection, I think we should watch each other's backs – I'm starting to feel like prey on this ship!' Jada said, indiscreetly turning her attention to a man not sitting far from them. Sarah turned to look and caught him just as he quickly turned his head away. She laughed.

'Deal,' she said, taking Jada's hand and shaking it.

For the next week the women were inseparable. They ate, played and toured the islands together. Sarah had never had so much fun and found she enjoyed Jada's company immensely.

'It's a pity I'm not a guy,' Sarah joked one afternoon as they lay sunbathing on her private balcony. Jada turned to look her directly in the eyes.

'If you were a guy you'd be pretty much wasting your time with me,' Jada said slowly.

Sarah blushed. 'Oh god Jada, I'm sorry, I didn't know,' she said feeling flustered.

Jada smiled. 'Not all lesbians look like -' she said.

'I didn't mean it like that!' Sarah said feeling embarrassed.

'Yes you did – you think all lesbians wear men's clothes with rolled up socks stuffed down their pants,' she said laughing.

'Hey,' Sarah said playfully, swinging her legs over the sun bed, 'you said that, not me.'

'Be honest – would you kiss another woman?' Jada suddenly asked seriously. Sarah thought for a moment before answering.

'If I was attracted to her,' she said slowly.

'Are you attracted to me?' Jada asked slipping off her sun bed and sitting next to Sarah.

'Erm...Yes...' she said, her breasts rose sharply a she drew in a breath.

'Do you want to kiss me?' Jada asked moving her face within inches of Sarah's.

'Yes,' she breathed huskily, and leaned forward.

Much later, as they lay in bed, bodies entwined

and basking in the afterglow of sexual pleasure, Jada stroked Sarah's hair away from her face.

'Are you sure you've never slept with a woman before?' she asked.

'Positive! Well, it has crossed my mind but I never thought I'd act on it.'

'Oh yeah, that's what they all say,' Jada said mockingly.

'Oh, so you have a habit of deflowering innocent straight women?' Sarah joked.

'After your performance tonight, I'd hardly call you innocent!' Jada said, obviously pleased with Sarah's skill in lovemaking.

'Oh, you haven't seen anything yet,' Sarah replied, rolling on top of Jada and kissing her passionately.

7

An attractive young receptionist with a mop of black curly hair looked up as Sarah walked in to Withers and Peterson solicitors.

'Good morning how can I help you?' she said in an impersonal professional tone.

'I'm here to see Joe.' Sarah replied.

'Is he expecting you?' she asked, her expression changing from bland to curious.

'I should think so, tell him it's his ex-wife.'

'Oh okay,' the receptionist said, losing her facade for a moment.

He is obviously sleeping with her, Sarah thought to herself.

'Mr Withers,' she said into the telephone, 'Ms,' she put her hand over the phone motioning Sarah to update her with her surname.

'Just tell him it's Sarah,' she said smiling sweetly.

'Sarah is at reception to see you,' she said a little tightly, 'okay,' she said, replacing the receiver. 'Mr Withers said you can go straight in. It's the first door on your left.' She pointed in the direction of his office and indiscreetly eyed her up and down.

'Thank you.' She leant near her so she could read the nametag on her suit jacket. 'Melanie,' she said as she pushed opened the glass door and made her way to Joe's office.

He was standing in front of a glass-topped desk when she entered. He looked a little older than the last time she had seen him. A few lines had taken residence on his forehead and his once lean body was looking a little bigger.

'Sarah - David mentioned you were coming in,' he said walking up to her, unaware if he should embrace her or shake her hand. He opted for neither, as she stood motionless.

'Joe,' she replied.

'I was shocked when David told me you were back. Is this just a fleeting visit or are you back for good?' he asked, gazing at her appreciatively. She was sexier than he remembered. Moreover, there was something else about her. Her presence was calm and relaxed unlike the last time he had seen her.

'Back for good it seems. I've managed to get Holly back into her old school; she'll be starting there in the new term.'

'Good, good,' he said clasping his hands together, 'and you look great,' he said flashing his trademark grin.

'Thanks,' she said, with no emotion in her voice.

She was there about their daughter and that was all that mattered, 'I'm here about Holly,' she said.

'You've been getting the maintenance payments haven't you?' he asked, looking confused.

'Yes,' she said, 'and they are very generous.'

'Oh good,' he said.

'I'm talking about when she going to see you?'

'Oh,' he said walking back behind his desk, 'please take a seat,' he said as though he was talking to a client.

She sat opposite him in a white leather chair.

'She's... um... how old now?' he asked trying desperately to pluck her age out of thin air.

'Eight,' Sarah said lightly.

'Of course - eight, bloody hell time flies doesn't it. So how is she?' he asked uncomfortably.

'She's fine but I think she'd be even better if she could see her dad.'

'Of course I want to see her,' he said slightly

flustered, 'these past few years have been so busy, what with me and David starting our own practice.'

'I can imagine Joe. I'm not here to talk about the past. I want to know what happens now.'

He looked a bit taken aback. The old Sarah was always very much interested in the past. That's what most of their arguments were about. He noticed that she had indeed changed. She was mellow, not like the wildcat he had been married to.

'Well, I'll check my diary and arrange a convenient time for us to meet,' he said, thinking how nice it would be to intimate with Sarah again. Whilst she was talking, he was thinking about all the things he would like to do to her and wondered if she'd be up for it.

'Anytime this week would be great,' Sarah was saying as he snapped out of his fantasy.

'This week... yes... I'm sure something can be arranged.' *God, she is beautiful,* he thought as he watched her breast rise and fall with each breath she took.

She stood up, 'so shall I tell Holly you'll be contacting her?'

'No, I'll surprise her... I promise I will call by the end of the week and arrange something with her. Do you want to leave me your number and I'll call her on that,' he said.

She wrote her number down and handed it to him.

She turned to leave. 'So she'll be seeing you soon.'

'Definitely,' he said, unable to get up from behind his desk. There was no way on earth that he would be able to hide his erection. 'See you soon,' he said as she walked out the door.

She still had that sexual energy about her that he had always found so irresistible. He was actually glad that she was back in town.

8

'Can you answer that?' Laura called out to David as she cracked two eggs into a frying pan. She heard him speaking for several minutes before entering the kitchen.

'Sit down, breakfast won't be a min,' she said as she turned the eggs over.

'I'll just have a cup of tea,' David said picking up the *Guardian* from the table.

'David, you need to eat darling. There's hardly anything of you as it is,' she said, placing a cup of tea in front of him and noticing his distraction. It seemed to be a permanent feature on his face lately.

'I'll get something at the office,' he said taking two mouthfuls of tea and placing it on the table.

'Who was on the phone?' Laura asked.

'Work,' he sighed. 'I'm going to work late again tonight, I've got an important meeting tomorrow so I need to go over some paperwork with Joe.'

'I feel like I never see you anymore,' Laura said, trying her hardest not to sound like a nagging wife. She was so proud of him and all that he had achieved and she understood that he was trying to establish his partnership with Joe, but she worried about the effects it seemed to be having on his health – and their relationship. He'd been looking pale lately and his suit hung loosely around his frame.

'I'll be as early as I can – it all depends how far I get,' he said, standing up. Taking his black suit jacket from the back of the chair, he slowly put his arm through it.

'Is your shoulder still playing up?' Laura asked, walking over him. She held his jacket while he eased into it.

'Now and again,' he said, grimacing as he finally got it on.

'You really need to go and see the doctor. What's the point of paying an extortionate amount on private medical care if we never use it?'

'Because I'm up to my eyeballs with work, and anyway I'm sure it's just the way I've been sleeping on it, nothing to worry about,' he said quickly, kissing the top of her head. As she began to protest, he turned her around to face the cooker. 'Your eggs are burning.' Whilst her attention was diverted, he slipped out of the kitchen and she heard the front door close seconds later.

'Has Dad left already?' James asked as he rushed into the kitchen.

'Yes, a few minutes ago. Did you want to speak with him about something?'

'Not really,' he said, taking his place at the table.

'You can talk to me, you know,' Laura said putting her hand on his shoulder.

'I know,' he said bashfully. 'Why'd he leave so early?' he asked, unable to hide his disappointment.

'Work,' she said, knowing it was a feeble answer. 'I tell you what though, why don't we all do something at the weekend?' she said, trying to sound cheerful.

'Yeah,' he said, unconvinced.

'We will, I promise,' she said, looking him in the eyes. 'We haven't been kayaking for a while. What say we go on Saturday?'

James brightened up. 'Do you really think Dad will be up for it?' he asked eagerly.

'Of course he will,' she said ruffling his hair. 'Why wouldn't he be – he loves being on the water.'

'He doesn't seem to want to do much with us these days.' James pouted.

'He's just tired darling, it's nothing to do with you.

Come on, eat your breakfast while I go and get your sister out the bathroom.' Laura hadn't realised that David being absent was having such an effect on James. She reminded herself to discuss it with him – whilst she understood he had work commitments, he also had a family.

The sound of the letterbox opening attracted her attention. Scooping to pick up the large envelope that had landed on the tiled floor she raised her brow, surprised to see it was addressed to her. *How strange*, she thought. Tearing open the seal, she withdrew a brochure about a diploma in Photojournalism. She certainly hadn't requested it and she wasn't, as far as she knew, on any mailing lists that would have indicated her interest in the subject. It must have been a coincidence.

She sat on the bottom step and flicked through it, sighing as she thought of what her life would have been like had she not dropped out university when she was pregnant with James. Photojournalism had been her lifelong dream. She'd been convinced that by the time she was thirty she would be at the top of her game and had fantasised about all the exotic locations she would have travelled to, the interesting articles she would have written, and the interesting people she would have met.

Something stirred within her as she read the module outlines and she found herself noting that the course was held over three mornings a week. She stood up suddenly, dismissing the thoughts of going to college as being silly. She was a mother and a wife now – that was her life, not a student running around chasing dreams. She absentmindedly put the brochure on the hallway table.

'If you're not downstairs in five minutes, you'll have to go to school without any breakfast,' she called up to Emily and walked into the kitchen feeling an odd sense of depression.

9

David sat in his office alone, staring out of the window. He'd thought of nothing but Laura all morning. He knew dwelling on the past and on happier times would not make his task any easier. When his mobile phone rang on his desk he picked it up immediately. His body relaxed and he smiled as he recognised the voice. He was glad she had phoned, but he spoke to her briefly.

'I've told Laura I've got a work thing later, so I can meet you around five…' Things were moving too fast, but he knew what he had to do. He left his office and walked the short distance to Joe's. Joe was speaking to a client on the phone so he took a seat opposite him and absentmindedly played with the knockers on his desk.

'What's up?' Joe asked when he hung up.

'I'm going to need some time off – starting immediately,' he said, looking his friend in the eyes.

'Yeah, right!' Joe said, laughing. 'You taking time off? Not in my lifetime,' he said as he shuffled through paperwork on his desk. David put his hand firmly on the papers, clamping them down to the desk.

'I'm serious, Joe,' he said. The smile disappeared from Joe's face.

'Is everything alright at home Dave? Is Laura okay - the kids?' he asked, concern spreading across his face.

'Everyone is fine,' David said, returning his hand to his lap now that he knew he had Joe's full attention.

'So what's brought this on then, is it because John Dee was put away yesterday?' Joe asked, puzzled by his friend's unusual behaviour.

'Partly, I just need a break,' he said matter-of-factly. 'You know I've been working since I was eighteen, and the only time I've had a break has been with Laura and the kids.'

'And that's hardly a break,' Joe said in agreement, remembering how stressful family holidays with the children had been. 'So how long you taking? A couple of weeks?' he asked. 'I can easily cover your workload.'

'It'll be longer than a few weeks,' David said, 'more like months.' Joe laughed out loud.

'I see,' he said in a conspiratorial tone. 'You're having a midlife crisis.'

David ignored his comment. 'I think it's for the best if you get a temp in to cover me, rather than you getting bogged down with my work. Everything's in order, so it shouldn't take someone more than a day to get up to speed with things.'

Joe stood up and walked around the table to his friend. 'What's brought all this on Dave?' he asked his tone serious and filled with concern.

'I just think I'm burnt out, John's case just pushed me over the edge,' he said, standing up and patting Joe on the shoulder. 'I just need a break from everything. Recharge my batteries so to speak,' he said with a smile that failed to reach his eyes.

Joe eyed him suspiciously. 'How are things going with Laura?' he asked.

David looked at Joe for a few seconds.

'Yes, fine, everything's fine,' he said walking towards the door. 'I'll work until the end of today.' Then he left, softly closing the door behind him.

***

It was early evening when David stepped through the doors of Clara's wine bar. Sally caught his eye – she was hard to miss with her frizzy auburn hair and red rimmed glasses.

'How have you been?' she asked once they were

seated.

'It's getting harder every day, living this lie,' he said. She put her hand on his reassuringly and he smiled at her tightly. A waiter appeared and took their drinks order and within a few minutes he was back, placing two tumblers of whiskey in front of them.

'Will you tell her tonight?' she asked patiently once they were alone again. He nodded then took a gulp of the amber liquid.

'Yes, I'll tell her tonight.' She smiled at him and their eyes locked in a mutual understanding. 'Thanks for being so patient with me,' he said. 'I must drive you crazy with the amount of times I've changed my mind. I know this will break her,' he said, more to himself than Sally. He squeezed his eyes shut as if trying to block out the image. 'But she'll get through it,' he continued.

'I've told Joe I'm taking a few months off.'

'How did he take it?'

'Fine. It'll be fine,' he said again. His hands were trembling as he lifted the glass to his lips. 'So, I've booked myself on a bit of an adventure holiday next month.' Sally sat back in her chair and watched David as he spoke animatedly about the places he would visit in the coming weeks. 'And then finally...' he said, 'I'll finish off with the Amazon.'

'I'm jealous,' she said smiling.

'You're more than welcome to join me,' he said genuinely.

'I would love to, more than anything,' she said, 'but...' she trailed off.

'Yes, I know,' he said flatly. He gulped down the remains of his drink. 'Well, I can't put this off any longer,' he said as he raised his hand to catch the waiter's attention.

'Will you call me tonight?' she asked.

'Yes, as soon as I've told her.'

10

Lost in distant memories, Laura didn't hear Emily enter the room. Curled up on the sofa, a photo album on her lap, Laura looked at old photographs of her late father.

'What you doing?' Emily asked as she knelt down next to her.

'Oh just looking at some photo's of your granddad,' she said, showing Emily the picture of her father standing tall and proud, Laura in his arms.

'You look like me,' Emily said, noticing the striking resemblance between them both.

'Yes I do don't I?'

'When was that picture taken?' Emily asked taking it from her mother's hand.

'A very long time ago, long before you were born.'

'You must have been very sad when Granddad died,' Emily said gazing down at the picture.

'I was, I still am, and when you lose someone you love it hurts very much.' It still brought a lump to her throat when she thought of her father.

'Is that why Nanny Patricia lives in another country?'

'I suppose so,' she said wearily.

'Did she stop loving Granddad when he died?'

'Oh no never,' she said. 'She loved my dad very much but when he died she didn't like being alone. It's like when Holly went away and you didn't see her, do you remember how sad you were?'

Emily nodded.

'And although she was your number one best friend you still made other friends, but no one could replace Holly.'

'Never,' Emily said.

'Well that's how it was with Nanny Patricia.'

'I wish she didn't live so far away.'

'I know darling, so do I.' Laura's mother had only returned to England twice since she had left. Their once close relationship had grown distant and they barely spoke at all anymore.

'That won't ever happen to us, will it?' Emily asked.

'What won't?'

'Dad leaving us.'

'Of course not,' she reassured her laughing. 'You're dad is a strong young man, he won't be going anywhere for a long, long time, you've got nothing to worry about there,' she said.

'Good.' Emily handed back the photograph.

'I want to live with you and Dad until you're a hundred,' she said.

'I think you'll want to leave home before then,' Laura laughed. 'By the time we're a hundred you'll be in your seventies and you may have had children of your own by then.'

Emily screwed her face up. 'Yuck, I'm never going to have children,' she said determinedly. 'I'm going to be an air hostess and travel the world.'

'What about when you fall in love?'

'I'm going to marry a pilot and we are going to get a dog and name him poodles and live happily ever after,' she continued caught up in her fantasy.

Life never turns out how you think it will, she wanted to tell her, but decided against it. Who was she to shatter her illusions?

11

David stood outside the front door for a long time before working up the courage to go inside. The sound of Laura and the children's laughter made him want to turn around and leave before they knew he was home, instead he forced himself to walk into the living room with arms wide open as the children ran into them.

'Dad, look what we've got,' James said, pushing the game box into his chest. He glanced helplessly at Laura.

'Drink?' she mouthed, not wanting to interrupt James. David nodded.

'I think we should play this now,' Emily said climbing up on David.

'You do, do you?' he said hugging her.

'Yes... because James thinks he's the best at everything and I told him he wouldn't be able to beat you,' she said proudly, hugging her father tightly. He closed his eyes, close to tears. Putting her back on the floor, he took his jacket off, and threw it on the armchair. Lowering himself onto the floor, he opened the board game and tried to distract himself.

'Right, where are the instructions for this then?' Laura returned with his drink and kissed him on the top of his head as she passed it to him.

'Thanks,' he said without looking up. He enjoyed playing with his children. It was a perfect moment – just a father having fun with his kids, but he felt like a fraud knowing that the next day it would all be shattered. This moment in time would be the last one they all shared as a happy family.

The next hour passed quickly and when it was time for the children to go to bed, he held them tightly to his chest, not wanting to let go. His throat constricted when they told him they loved him.

'I love you too,' he said in a croaky voice as Laura took them upstairs to settle them down. Minutes later, she re-joined him, a glass of wine in her hand. She had barely sat down next to him when he spoke.

'I'm leaving you, Laura,' he said – so quietly that she barely heard him.

'What did you say?' she asked in disbelief, putting her glass on the coffee table. With all the strength in his body, he managed to turn and look directly at her.

'I'm leaving you,' he repeated. She stared at him, stunned and grief stricken.

'Is this some kind of joke?' she asked. 'Because if it is, it's bloody well not funny.' She stood up, adrenaline coursing through her body. David looked at her, wanting desperately to hold her in his arms and make her feel secure and safe – to take back the words that had unceremoniously left his mouth and shattered her world. Seconds passed but they felt like an eternity. Telling her he was leaving was the only part he had ever gotten to when he'd acted out this scene in his head – he didn't know where to go from there. He wished the ground would just swallow him up whole.

Laura was dumbstruck. She felt as though her lips had been glued together. Her mind was racing. So he *was* having an affair. All this time she had tried to think the best of him – she'd had so much faith in him, even feeling sorry for him, when all the time he'd actually been seeing someone else! Suddenly feeling unsteady, she sat down again. 'I'm sorry,' he said, his voice coarse with emotion.

'Is that it?' she finally managed to whisper. 'You're sorry?' She laughed bitterly. He took a deep breath.

'Look, I know this is not the best time to be telling

you this, but I've taken indefinite leave from the office. I'm going travelling for a while,' he said. She stared up at him.

'What?' she asked, confused.

'I...'

She interrupted him quickly. 'I heard what you said,' she said, still in shock, 'but I can't quite get my head around it.' She stood up to face him. 'Let me get this right...' she said, shaking her head in disbelief. 'You've left your job to go travelling – and while you're at it you're leaving me and the kids as well. Is that about it?'

He stood up and took her hands in his.

'I know it sounds bad when you put it like that,' he said, 'but this is something I need to do.'

'What,' she said, pushing him away. 'You need to leave me and the kids.' It was more of a statement than a question.

'I know you can't understand this...' Before he could continue, she exploded.

'You're bloody well damn right I can't understand this. Jesus Christ David, have you lost your senses?' she cried incredulously, her face contorted with rage.

'No, Laura,' he said softly, 'I've come to them.'

Laura stood still, unable to move, unable to believe what she was hearing. His words were not fully connecting with her brain. She was unaware of how much time had passed as they both stood there looking at each other. She was not an overly emotional woman, if she hurt she internalised it, but at that moment in time she desperately wished that she was the total opposite. She wanted to scream, to plead, to beg – but something inside her held her back.

'Are you seeing someone else?' she asked him, dreading to hear the answer. She needed to know that there was some reason for him to shatter their lives like this. 'Just tell me the truth,' she said flatly.

'No, I'm not seeing anyone else,' he finally said, shifting his feet.

'I don't believe you,' she said running her hand through her hair. He shrugged his shoulders. He had a sudden urge to get out of the living room – to get away from her. He started to feel sick and swallowed down on the vomit that was threatening. David hated emotional dramas, and more than that, he hated hurting people, Laura especially, but now he had to put his needs first.

'I just need some time on my own.'

'You need some time on your own?' She shook her head in amazement. 'What, do you think I don't feel like that, that I don't feel like running away sometimes?' she asked him. 'But I don't, because I made a commitment to you for life, not just until I couldn't be bothered anymore.'

'Laura, I love you and the kids more than anything – one day you'll understand,' he said, burying his hands in his pockets so she couldn't see them shaking.

'Then why?' she nearly screamed. 'Please explain why you are leaving if you love us so much.' He wouldn't look her in the eyes, his head drooped dejectedly.

'I wish I could explain it but I can't,' he said regretfully.

'Can't or won't,' Laura retorted. The talented solicitor who made a living out of speaking stood in front of her speechless.

'I think you should leave now,' Laura heard a voice say. It took a moment to realise it was hers. David stepped towards her and she put out her hand to stop him. 'David, just go. I'll go over to Sarah's tomorrow, you can come and pack your stuff then. I don't want the children to see you leaving.'

'What are you going to tell them?' he asked weakly. Laura rounded on him in fury.

'What do you want me to tell them? That you grew tired of being a husband and a father and decided to do all the things you felt you missed out on?' she said.

'You wouldn't tell them that,' he said, shocked.

'No David, I wouldn't, I couldn't be that cruel.' Laura picked up his jacket and handed it to him. He reached his hand out slowly to take it.

'I know you don't believe me Laura but...' He looked pale and unsure of himself. She put her hand up.

'Save it for someone who wants to hear your bullshit David, you're not in court now.' She walked to the front door and opened it. Seconds later David followed her, still trying to speak.

'Don't speak to me,' she hissed, 'just go.' The will to fight had gone out of her. He walked out the door leaving her to adapt to a world that he had just turned upside down.

Shutting the door behind him Laura slid to the floor, biting down on her fist to keep her cries from being heard. How could she have not seen this coming? The late nights, the excessive amount of time spent in the bathroom getting ready for work, talking secretively to someone on the phone. It had been staring her in the face but she had not dared believe, she hadn't wanted to believe it.

She was still sitting crumpled in a ball on the floor when hours later, daylight streamed through the glass pane. She fought to pull herself together when she heard the children making their way to the bathroom to bathe and brush their teeth. She would not let them find her like this, she could break down whilst they were at school. She checked herself in the hallway mirror and was horrified at what stared back at her – swollen; blood-shot eyes were covered with black smears where her eyeliner and mascara had run. Her hair was matted and her clothes were crumpled. She quickly went into the downstairs toilet and splashed water on her face before using the soap to wash away the black marks. She ran a brush through her hair and went to get a clean top from the utility room. By the time James and Emily were in the kitchen waiting for breakfast she had miraculously performed a complete makeover.

'Is Dad coming to watch me play football tonight?' James asked as he wolfed down his cereal.

'I don't know darling, I'll ring him later,' Laura said fighting to keep her voice steady.

'Okay,' he said, dropping a piece of cereal on the floor for Ninja, who crunched it in his mouth.

'James, I've told you not to feed the cat from the table,' Laura said with her back to him, lacking her usual conviction.

'Sorry Mum,' he said disingenuously, smirking at Emily and dropping another. Emily clasped her hand to her mouth trying to muffle her giggles.

'I know what you're doing, James.' Laura turned quickly, nearly catching him in the act.

'What?' he asked innocently, widening his eyes. Laura couldn't help but laugh. The children joined in and Ninja purred, happy and contented.

12

Dropping the children off at school, Laura immediately called Sarah.

'Can I come over?' she said before Sarah had a chance to greet her, 'I don't want to talk about it over the phone,' Laura continued, battling to keep the tears at bay.

'Of course you can, I'll put the kettle on.'

'I'm going to need something a lot stronger than tea,' Laura said before ringing off. Before she drove off she texted David to tell him that he had until three to move his belongings from the house and that James had a football match that evening. Whether he attended or not was his prerogative, she had kept her promise to James. As much as she was hurting she wanted to minimise the pain they were going to feel once they found out the father they adored had left them.

It wasn't long before she sat in Sarah's kitchen nursing a shot of vodka.

'Nice place,' Laura said, glancing around the apartment.

'It will do until the house is ready, the lease is up in a couple of months, I can't wait to move back home. So what's happened that we're sitting here drinking vodka at nine in the morning?'

Laura sipped the alcohol, her face distorting as the liquid warmed her insides.

'David left me last night,' she finally managed to say.

Sarah closed her eyes, inhaled deeply, and sighed. Her insides churned at the thought of what Laura was going through and what she still had to face. She reached out and put her arms around Laura, gently rocking her.

'I'm sorry,' Sarah said, her voice husky and

emotional.

'I don't think it's quite sunk in yet,' Laura said. She felt like crying but the tears just wouldn't come. She felt numb, like this was happening to someone else.

'He said there's no one else,' she laughed angrily, 'can you believe it, that David, the great man of honour, would just get up and go one day, just like that. I don't know why he let it get to the point where he thought it was beyond repair before he told me how he felt. I never took David for someone who couldn't talk about how he was feeling. This is all so out of character, I still can't believe that this is happening,' she said, taking a gulp of vodka.

'Look at me, Laura,' Sarah said, holding her face in her hands. 'I know you don't think so at this moment but you have got to believe me, you will get through this, you will,' she said adamantly.

'I don't want to get through anything, I just want my life back the way it was.' The tears finally began to course down her cheeks.

Sarah went to fetch a tissue and then dabbed the tears away.

'And what if he doesn't want to come back, Laura, then what?' she said softly.

'Of course he'll want to come back – he has a wife and children. He's just having a midlife crisis, what with the pressures from work and everything, he'll realise what he's missing in a few days...'

'I thought the same thing with Joe,' Sarah said.

'That's not the same. David loves me,' she said, instantly regretting it. She put her hand to her mouth in shock. 'Sarah, I'm so sorry, that was a horrible thing to say, please forgive me,' she said, looking forlorn, fresh tears welling in her eyes.

Sarah smiled at her without any anger or

resentment.

'I know you didn't mean any malice Laura,' she said kindly, 'and there's nothing wrong with speaking the truth. You're right – Joe never loved me. Perhaps if I'd faced up to the truth at the time I wouldn't have gotten into the mess I did and I wouldn't have put him in a position he had no wish to be in.' She poured herself a cup of coffee. 'Laura, if David wants to come back it should be because he wants to, not because he was forced to under duress.'

'How has this even got to this stage?' Laura asked, still in denial. 'How does someone who loved you so much and was so in the relationship, just stop?' She clicked her fingers. 'Just like that... it's over.'

'That's something only David can answer.'

'He didn't say he wanted a divorce, that's what makes me think that it's just a blip he's going through. He's always been so responsible for us all for so long, maybe he just wants to kick back for a few weeks without the baggage of family life,' Laura said hopefully.

'Have you told James and Emily yet?' Sarah asked. Laura shook her head.

'I wouldn't know where to begin.'

'I would offer my help but the way Emily feels about me at the moment I'm the last person she'd want around when you deliver that kind of blow to her.'

'I don't see the point in telling them yet, especially as he might change his mind and come home – I don't want to cause them grief over nothing, you know...' A thought suddenly hit her. 'He could be suffering from depression - that would explain a lot of his behaviour lately...' Her mood began to lift slightly.

'And what if it isn't depression?' Sarah said persistently. 'What if he *has* left and isn't ever coming back. Then what? I agree James and Emily need to be protected,' Sarah said, trying to tread carefully in delicate waters, 'but they also have the right to honesty,' she said. 'They aren't stupid, they'll pick up the vibe that something's wrong sooner or later, even if you tell them he's gone away on business for a while.'

Laura's mobile vibrated, indicating she had a text message. She read it quickly.

'It's from David,' she said. 'He's moved all his clothes from the house and left the house keys in the kitchen,' she said, 'and he's coming round tonight to tell the kids,' she continued, stunned. 'This is for real, isn't it?' she asked Sarah, her bottom lip trembling. 'I'm so scared... I don't think I can do this alone.'

'You're not alone Laura, that's why I'm here.' Sarah stood up decisively. 'Let me get showered and dressed and I'll come over to your place with you,' she said, not wanting Laura to be by herself when she walked back into the house. She knew full well how oppressive a silent house could be.

***

'Why did I have to miss my game tonight?' James asked Laura, obviously displeased.

'Your dad and I have something we need to tell you,' Laura said, stroking James's hair. Both children looked at each other to see if either one of them knew what this was to do with.

'We haven't done anything wrong,' Emily said, annoyed.

'Nobody said you had,' Laura said, smiling at her.

The doorbell rang.

'That'll be your dad now.'

'He's lost his keys again!' James said as he got up to open the front door. David and James entered the room together.

'Hi Dad,' Emily said walking over to him and hugging his waist.

'Hello squirt,' he said squeezing her shoulder.

His stomach was in knots.

'Kids, take a seat please,' Laura said. As she waited for them to be seated, she looked at David. He looked tired and stressed, his morning shadow dark on his face. The children waited expectantly.

'There isn't an easy way to tell you both this,' David began, 'um...well...' He stalled, placing his thumb and finger on the bridge of his nose, his eyes obviously agitated.

'What is it, Dad?' James asked, his blue eyes looking at him full of innocence.

'Well, it's me and your mum,' David said looking at her. Laura shot David an icy stare, warning him not to make her any part of this.

'We...' he said unsteadily, '...I...I have to move out...'

'What!' both children cried simultaneously, looking confused.

'I'm going through some stuff at the moment,' he said a bit more confidently, 'and I think it's best if I move out to deal with it,' he said finally, evidently relieved the worst was over. He had told them – now it was time for the aftermath. James started to cry while Emily glared at him as her mind processed what he'd just said.

'Don't you want to live with us anymore?' James asked between sobs.

'Oh James,' David said, his heart breaking, 'this has got nothing to do with you or Emily.'

Charming, Laura thought. *Don't make it too obvious it's me that you can't bear to be with.*

'We still love you, nothing is going to change. We will both always be there for you,' David said, consoling him.

It's always the children who suffer, Laura thought, watching her stunned children's faces crumple with sorrow. Emily got up and stood by her mother's side, taking her hand. It was an act of defiance – she was letting her father know on which side of the fence she was sitting. So many of her friends at school had told her that their dads had left their mums. She believed her dad was different and he would never leave them, that's what her mum had told her anyway. Dry-eyed she watched James as he became hysterical.

'Then why?' James had fallen on his knees in front of his father. 'Please don't go, Dad,' he begged, tears streaming down his face, 'I'll be good all the time,' he said, trying to bargain with him. 'I'll take the rubbish out without being told to,' he said, desperately trying to think of all his bad habits that annoyed David. 'I won't annoy Emily anymore, I promise!'

David stood up, the excruciating atmosphere becoming unbearable.

'Mum, please tell him to stay,' he said, curling his body around David's legs and holding them tight. David bent down and tried several times to unlock James's grip.

'James,' he said in a firm voice, 'stop it.' When this did not yield a response, he said louder still, 'James! Stop it!' He yanked at James's wrists and managed to break free. Laura went over to James and knelt down beside him, stroking his hair off his face. She looked up at David, trying to meet his gaze, but he continued to look away, brushing off her anguished looks.

'Just go, David,' she said as he stood there mutely, like someone observing a horrific car crash. 'Just go!'

she said again, this time screaming at the top of her lungs. Her pitch seemed to shake him out of the trance he was in. A dejected David walked past Emily, her hurt eyes burning a hole in his back as he strode through the door.

'Noooooooo!' James screamed as front door slammed shut. 'Dad... noooooooo!' Laura held out her arm for Emily to join her on the floor with James while she tried to soothe him.

13

A few weeks had passed since David had left the family home and Laura still couldn't believe that he had actually gone. She was still convinced he would return and that he was just having a midlife crisis. He had little contact with her since he left and so when her mobile phone bleeped with a message from him she couldn't help feeling hopeful.

> **I have leased an apartment,**
> **should be settled in by weekend,**
> **can kids come and stay?**

Her heart froze. *What the hell was going on?* she thought as she frantically text him back.

> **Y have you done that?**
> **U have a home!**
> **What is this all about?**

Seconds later another bleep on her phone.

> **Said all I have to say!**
> **can kids come at**
> **weekend?**

Sighing, she reluctantly texted back.

> **Fine have it ur way**
> **I can't believe ur doing**
> **this 2 us :(**

Laura was so confused. Had she missed vital signs that would have told her that David was unhappy? Had she been a bad wife? Had she not been attentive enough to his needs? She had given everything she had to him and it was obviously not enough. She had mistakenly thought they had the most amazing relationship.

She pulled the covers up to her chest. She couldn't bring herself to get up. Sarah kept telling her to find her inner strength but she was convinced she didn't have any.

'You will get through this... and the pain will lessen, I promise you,' Sarah said, *'but, you've just got to try, let the grief knock you down but then find the strength to get up again. No one can help you Laura, you have got to do this by yourself. Your marriage might be over but your life isn't.'*

'How do you expect me to just accept that ten years of my life has been for nothing. That my husband is now a threat to everything I have held sacred.'

'Laura, you have two beautiful children, it hasn't been for nothing.'

'You know David always sorted out the finances.' Sarah nodded.

'Well he sent me an email informing me that I had better take over all the accounts because it was yet another pressure he didn't need. I wouldn't even know where to bloody start.'

'I'll help you, but sooner or later you're going to have to stand on your own two feet.'

Sarah pleaded with Laura to see the counsellor she had seen when she had separated from Joe, but Laura insisted she did not need a counsellor – she just needed David.

***

Laura stared long and hard at the phone. Every

time she went to dial David's number, she stopped herself. She needed to speak to him desperately but she was scared he would reject her again. Throwing caution to the wind, she quickly pressed his mobile number on speed dial. It rang several times before he answered.

'Is everything all right?' he asked straight away.

'Yes, everything's fine, considering the circumstances.' She paused. 'David?'

'Yes?' he said. He sounded like he was in bed.

'Are you at home?' she asked him.

'Um, yeah… why?' At that moment she heard a woman's voice start to speak, then abruptly stop. She could hear David putting his hand over the mouthpiece. 'Look, now's not a good time Laura, is it important?' he asked in a hushed voice.

'No David, it's not... I'm sorry to bother you,' she said, and hung up the phone. It rang straight away and she snatched it up, thinking it was David calling back to explain why a woman was at his place, but the voice on the other end of the phone was unfamiliar.

'Mrs Peterson?' the formal voice asked.

'Yes, speaking. Who is this?'

'Mr Picard, James's headmaster.'

'Hello Mr Picard, is everything alright?' she asked, panicking.

'Well, no, no it's not I'm afraid,' he said, sounding disappointed. 'I'd like you to come and collect James straight away. I have given him a week's suspension for fighting on school grounds.'

'What!' Laura sounded incredulous. He cleared his throat.

'I said I'd like you to....'

'I'll be there right away,' she said, thinking to herself what a pompous arse Mr Picard was. She drove to the school as quickly as she could and made her way to the headmaster's office. She felt a little nervous herself, as if she were the one in trouble. She saw James sitting outside the headmaster's door, clothes scuffed, blood on his shirt, his head hung down, whether in shame or anger she couldn't tell.

'James,' she said quietly as she approached him. He looked up at her, his beautiful innocent eyes looked wounded.

'Where's Dad?' he asked

'At work,' she lied.

'Like he would have come anyway,' he said, the hurt apparent in his voice. She attempted to touch him but he shoved her hand away. His behaviour was so out of character it frightened her. Who had replaced her loving, affectionate, charming, son with this angry little person? Mr Picard opened his door.

'Ahh, so you've arrived,' he said, as if she'd taken an hour to get there, not the ten minutes it actually took.

'What happened?' she asked, standing up straight, determined not to be intimidated by this bully of a man. She was in a mother's protective mode and nothing could make her cower.

'Please step in my office,' he said, his attitude mellowing as if he sensed a change in her.

'I won't be a minute, darling,' she said to James. He didn't respond as he stared aimlessly out of the window.

The headmaster explained that James had attacked another child who had been teasing him because his father no longer lived at home. She made all the appropriate noises he wanted to hear and she was relieved when he finally stood up.

'I will get my secretary to send you the letter of suspension by post,' he said as he led her to the door.

'You do that,' she replied as she walked back into

the corridor. 'Let's go James.' He picked up his bag huffily and obediently followed her to the car, slumping in the back seat.

'School's finished in ten minutes,' she said looking at him through the mirror, 'we may as well wait for Emily to come out.' They sat in silence for a few minutes. 'Do you want to talk about it?' she asked him.

'No,' he said moodily. Emily got into the car and quietly closed the door.

'Did you have a good day?' Laura asked, trying to be sociable.

'No,' was the one word answer. She watched as Emily slid her earphones on.

'Put your seat belts on,' she said to both of them. James slid the belt sulkily across himself and leaned across Emily to put hers on, as she hadn't heard her mother. Laura had not seen what had taken place but they began to scuffle in the back seat.

'Pack it in, you two,' she said, but they carried on. 'I said, pack it in!' Laura said firmly. James pinched Emily and she let out a loud scream and began to cry. The sudden eruption between James and Emily caused Laura's insides to rumble like a volcano. Her eyes blazed and her lips trembled. When she couldn't hold it in any longer, all of her circuits finally blew.

'Stop it... just stop it,' she yelled in a blind fury, 'I don't need this, do you hear me, I don't need you two bloody bickering like a pair of toddlers, don't you care how I feel? What I'm going through?' She began crying uncontrollably, banging her fist on the steering wheel in frustration. Inside, she was screaming for mercy.

Emily stared at her mother crying helplessly in the front seat. James began to cry next to her, covering his face with his hand.

'We're sorry Mum,' Emily said softly.

What am I doing? Laura thought, straightening herself up and wiping the tears away from her face. She turned around to look at them. James was curled up in the corner of his seat sobbing. Emily looked at her, shell-shocked. *What was she doing to her two innocent children?* The ones, she as a mother, was meant to protect. They looked empty.

'Emily you have nothing to apologise for,' she said her voice shaking. She stroked her cheek. 'Please forgive me,' she said, and reached over and took James's hand.

'James, look at me.' He slowly revealed his tear stained face. 'Your dad may have gone but we are still a family. I haven't been on the ball lately but I promise that's all going to change from today, okay?' she said with a new sense of purpose. He nodded weakly.

As soon as they arrived home, she put the car in neutral and James and Emily got out and ran up the steps to the house. James unlocked the front door and they went to their bedrooms.

Laura went straight to the phone and called David again, but this time she was not the emotional wreck she had been earlier – she had the spirit of a warrior. He answered straight away.

'Laura...' he started to say, but she cut him off.

'This isn't a social call,' she said with fiery conviction. 'I've just collected James from school – he's been suspended for a week for attacking another boy. This split is obviously affecting him a lot harder than I thought, I think you need to come round and have a word with him, today.' There was silence for a few moments.

'I can't make it today,' he said sheepishly. It was like a verbal slap in the face.

'What do you mean you can't make it? Our son needs you David, for Christ sake if you want to punish me for some unknown reason go ahead, but please don't make the children suffer.'

'I just can't Laura, maybe in a couple of days.'

'Fuck you and fuck your couple of days,' she shouted angrily, fire raging in her belly. She rang off and immediately dialled Sarah's number. When she answered, Laura spoke in a confident tone, her voice strong.

'Sarah, text me the number for that counsellor before something terrible and irrevocable happens. That bastard may have nearly broken me... but *he will not,*' she emphasised, 'break my children.'

14

'Mrs Peterson,' the receptionist called, 'Dr Leigh will see you now. It's your first door on the right,' she said smiling. Laura followed her directions along the blue carpeted corridor and was soon knocking gently on the counsellor's door. Within seconds, a woman small in stature, with a neat modest figure, had opened it. Her dark hair parted down the middle and was rolled up neatly on both sides.

'Ahh, Mrs Peterson,' she said, firmly shaking her hand. Her voice was soft and gentle, instantly putting Laura at ease.

'Please, call me Laura,' she said.

'Laura it is then,' she said, totally attentive to her, 'Please, take a seat,' she said, pointing to a brown and cream two-seater sofa.

The women started with small talk about the journey down to London and about life living in Bournemouth.

'It must be wonderful being surrounded by so much natural beauty,' Dr Leigh said wistfully.

'Yes, yes it is, I feel very lucky.'

'Good. Now, back to the reason you are here today. I'll quickly run through the way I do things so you know what to expect from me. I offer two counselling sessions to begin with and I'm hoping that through these sessions you will build a strong foundation to grow from, for you to stand firmly. I cannot cure you, all I can do is guide you. Are you happy with this so far?'

'Yes,' Laura said.

'Good, the first session, which will take place today, will go through the sort of support you said you needed when you filled out the questionnaire in the waiting room.' Laura nodded. 'Were there any questions that you'd like to ask me about?'

'No,' said Laura.

'Okay, great,' Dr Leigh said, retrieving the questionnaire. 'So I see that you've ticked "letting go" as the main thing you would like to discuss today – if it's okay with you, can you fill me in on what brings you here that relates to letting go?'

'Well...' Laura started slowly, 'my husband left me out of the blue. There were no outward signs that things were going wrong, and I'm suffering because I can't get him out of my mind. I never thought in a million years that David would betray me – would ever stop loving me and the more I think about him, the worse I feel and I can't function. I need him to function – I feel as though we've let our children down.'

'The first thing we must explore is addiction,' Dr Leigh said.

'Oh, no, I don't have any addictions,' Laura said hurriedly, thinking perhaps Dr Leigh had misunderstood.

'What I want you to do is look at the list I've written on this pad,' she said handing it over to Laura, 'and read what is written as though the words were said by someone else.' Laura scanned the list.

'Do those words come across as someone who is withdrawing from an addiction, or someone who's had a healthy, balanced life?'

Laura's eyes stared at the array of words on the paper: *need, can't live without, can't function, need him to function...*

'Are they not the words people use when they're talking about an addiction, whether it's alcohol, drugs, food, sex, shopping, or even... ' She paused. 'Love?' she added softly. 'People find that without their fix, life is not worth living, hence the need to consume more of it.'

Think about it logically, Laura. If you can reduce your own addiction to love, you can also reduce the suffering it's causing in your life. You've become dependent on your addiction, in this case your husband, and your whole sense of identity now depends on him. Without him, you feel like nothing. From here on in, if you want to survive, you have to take control of your life back,' she said with conviction in her voice.

'But how?' Laura asked weakly.

'By being independent of your husband. I don't mean financially – I mean personally. The place that you find yourself in now is the result of your own actions. You cannot blame anything on your husband or, for that matter, anyone else. You cannot make someone else responsible for your happiness or sadness – no one should have that power over your emotions but you. This is the first thing you have to accept Laura, that you are the captain of your own ship. Without acknowledging this, your addiction will be impossible to break and you'll always be dependent on someone, or something, to give you that fix.'

The session was soon finished – the hour had flown by. Laura's head felt tizzy. Looking at David like an addiction not only made sense, but she realised that it was also true. She'd been using David like a crutch to get through life. Was it any wonder that when he'd left, her whole world had become unbalanced.

***

Later that evening, Laura went over to Sarah's for dinner. James and Emily were excited they were going to be staying the night and Emily had been playfully teasing James about his crush on Holly: something he vehemently denied, but Laura had seen the glint in his eyes when they were together. How was such a seemingly innocent emotion such as love capable of becoming a weapon?

When they arrived, Jada had just finished setting the table. She welcomed her warmly and hugged her.

'How did your day go?' she asked, referring to her counselling session.

'Well, she certainly gave me food for thought,' she said as Sarah joined them.

'Hello, darling,' she said, kissing Laura on her cheek. 'So you met the infamous Dr Leigh.'

'I certainly did,' Laura said. 'It was an *experience*, I'll say that much.'

'Okay kiddies,' Sarah said turning around to the children. 'Who wants chicken nuggets and chips?'

'We do,' they said in unison.

'Well come and get it,' she said dividing the food onto their plates. 'We're ordering an Indian takeaway when the kids have settled down – you look like you're in need of a horrific amount of calories to be honest,' Sarah said, looking at the loose-fitting clothes Laura wore.

'I know,' she said, touching her stomach and feeling her ribs poking through. 'I'm starting my five meals a day eating plan tomorrow,' she said.

'I'm glad to hear it; otherwise we were plotting to start force feeding you!' she said looking at Jada, who nodded in agreement.

'Mum, can we go and play my Wii when we've finished?'

'Of course you can, darling,' she said.

After the children had finished dinner, they retired to Holly's bedroom. Settling beside her friend on the sofa, Sarah looked at Laura, concern in her eyes.

'So are you going to see her again?' she asked.

'Most definitely,' she said. 'The things she said are

so obvious but for some reason you just don't think of it yourself.'

'I know what you mean... I like the fact that she doesn't pretend she can cure your ailments or that she has a prescription pad waiting to zone you out.'

'The techniques are simple but so effective – when I realised David was leaving today to go travelling, instead of freaking out, I just kept concentrating on my breathing in order not to think about it. I'm not saying it worked all day but it allowed me some breathing space – some time when I wasn't feeling completely manic! It felt good to have a little bit of control back.'

'It gets better,' Sarah said. 'The more you practise the better you feel.'

'So, are you totally over Joe now, then?'

'Yes, totally – not that there was anything to really get over. I wasn't grieving for him when it came down to it, I was mourning for myself – the person I had lost in trying to become someone I wasn't.'

'Do you think you'll ever marry again?' she asked.

'Yes, most definitely,' she said looking at Jada. 'If she asks, that is...'

'Maybe,' Jada said, smiling. Laura shot up in her chair.

'Are you two...'

'Together?' Sarah laughed. 'Yes, we're together.'

Laura only just stopped her mouth dropping open.

'Oh my god, all this time and I didn't even know you were into women,' she said.

'A girl has to have some secrets,' she replied.

'I'm so surprised,' she said and quickly glanced at Jada. 'No offence to you.'

'None taken,' Jada replied smiling.

'But you were always into... boys, well men, why didn't you say anything before now?' she said, poking her playfully. 'You really are a dark horse. What other secrets are you keeping from me?' she joked.

'None, now don't start getting all paranoid on me,' Sarah said digging her back.

'Are you telling me we could have been together all this time,' Laura said, jokingly winking at Jada.

'Could you imagine?' Jada mused.

'Hey, what are you trying to imply? I think I'd make a pretty good catch... So, does Joe know?'

'If at any time he needs to know I'll tell him, but I'd rather not have to deal with the drama of Joe and his over-inflated ego.'

15

'So young lady what'd you want to do for your birthday?'

'I'm not fussed really,' Holly said keeping her eyes down.

'You don't expect me to believe that do you,' Sarah said gently tilting her face upwards, 'you love your birthday. Do you want to have a party?' she asked.

'No really Mum, I don't want to make any fuss.'

'Do I hear talk of a birthday party?' Jada said as she entered the room. Though only modestly dressed in black skinny jeans and a black jacket, she looked stunning the way the clothes moulded to her body.

'Well I thought it would be a good idea but it seems Holly has grown out of her birthday,' Sarah said.

'Grown out of it?' Jada said exaggerating. 'I'm thirty and I still get butterflies on my birthday,' she said brightly, taking her jacket off and throwing it on the arm of the sofa.

'I think I'll go and finish my home work,' Holly said solemnly and left the room.

'What was that about?' Jada asked lowering her voice.

'I don't really know. I'm wondering if it's being back in Bournemouth that's unsettling her, she hasn't been her normal self lately.'

'How about we give her a surprise party?' Jada said excitedly.

'Somehow I don't think she'd appreciate that,' she said ruefully. 'Holly hates surprises and she would never forgive me for going behind her back. If she says she doesn't want any fuss, then I'll abide by her wishes.'

'Okay,' Jada said, 'you're the mummy.' Feeling

slighted she switched the kettle on and took two cups out of the cupboard.

'Jada I didn't mean it like that. I'm not pulling a parental rights moment, I just don't want to do anything that will rock the boat at the moment.'

'And having a party for her will be rocking the boat how exactly?' Jada asked pouring the boiling water over herbal tea bags and placing the cup in front of Sarah.

'Because it will seem like I'm overriding her wishes. You don't understand what I was like before, I always did things I wanted to do for her, not because she wanted to do them, I was just pleasing myself,' she said sadly. 'I loved nothing better than being able to boast about what I'd done for Holly. Acting like the perfect mother, or so I thought. When Joe left, I did the worst possible thing a mother could do, I made her believe that Joe had left *us*. I never once said to her that Joe had left me. Which is what he had done.'

'Come on Sarah you're being a bit harsh on yourself,' Jada said kindly as she sat on the bar stool at the kitchen Island.

'No,' Sarah said shaking her head. 'No I'm not, believe me I'm not; she was six years old when he left Jada, a mere child, she didn't understand why her dad had left. It was my responsibility to protect her. And I didn't, I just made an already bad situation worse. For months she wouldn't let me out of her sight. She always needed to know where I was and what time I'd be back and do you know what the sick thing is?'

Jada shook her head.

'I loved her neediness. I loved the fact that she needed me.' Sarah bowed her head in shame.

'Sarah many people, if not most people have children out of the need to feel needed, to try to make sense out of their life. You're not the monster you are trying to make out you are.'

'Do you think that makes it okay, to bring an innocent child into the world and burden it with problems it has no business knowing. Jesus, she'll have enough of her own problems to deal with by the time she reaches adulthood. I should have told her the truth - that Joe left because he didn't love *me*,' she said. 'Now I'm trying to rectify what I did. That is by giving her a voice and respecting her boundaries and, within reason, her wishes.'

'I didn't know you felt like that,' Jada said.

'I've put the past in the past now, I just don't want to make any unavoidable mistakes. It's not that hard, I just tend to think more about how my actions will affect her and so far it seems to be working.'

'You have been doing a great job with Holly,' Jada said reassuringly.

'We'll see,' she said. 'So - I hope you understand now that I wasn't trying to play down your suggestion.'

'Now that you've explained you're reasoning behind it, how could I not. So what are you going to do for her then?' she asked at a loss for what to do.

'I'll ask her if she wants to do something with Emily and James. Maybe we can take them out to Alton towers or something.'

'Sounds good,' Jada said. 'Since you're in a bare your soul mood, is now a good time to bring up what's been on my mind lately.'

'Jada, you can talk to me any time about *anything,*' she said raising her eyebrow.

'You're incorrigible,' Jada said shaking her head. 'Seriously though, what's going to happen about Joe?'

'I have told Joe where he can reach his daughter if he wishes to. I can't do much more than that, I'm not going to hold a gun to his head, at the end of the day it's his choice,' she said.

'What do you think he'll do?'

'Knowing Joe, nothing until it suits him. If he hasn't made any effort in the past two years to contact her I'm not exactly expecting a miracle now. He said he'd be in touch by now and he hasn't, so what can I do?' she said shrugging her shoulders. 'Why'd you ask anyway?'

'I was thinking how hard it must be for her being back and not having heard from him. It must be tough.'

They both turned to the door when it opened and Holly appeared looking somewhat brighter.

'Mum, I've decided I will have a party but only a very small one, maybe just with Emily and James. I don't want a big fuss.'

'If that's what you want darling,' Sarah said.

'Yep.'

'Have you finished your homework?'

'Nearly, I'm just going to make a sandwich and then I'll get back to it.'

'Do you want me to make one for you?' Jada said rising from her chair.

'No thanks, I'll make it,' she said smiling at Jada. 'I can make you one too if you like.'

'Come to think of it I am pretty peckish,' she said, 'I'll have whatever you're having then.'

'Do you want one mum?'

'No thanks. I know what concoctions you put between pieces of bread,' she said smiling at her.

'I think her sandwiches are pretty inventive,' Jada said as Holly gathered the foodstuff from the fridge and cupboard.

'If peanut butter and banana sandwiches rock your boat who am I to argue,' she smiled at her. She took her black leather jacket off and hung it on the back of a chair.

Jada looked at her with sudden intensity. The one shoulder top Sarah was wearing exposed her perfectly shaped bare shoulder. Jada would often just become in awe of Sarah's beauty and presence and would ache to be in her arms. Sarah noticed the look on Jada's face and returned it, her own longing evident in her eyes.

'I've done it,' Holly said breaking their spell. 'Cheese salad...'

'Oh lovely.' Jada said before Holly finished her sentence.

'With peanut butter,' she added, smiling up at her.

'oh, er – great,' Jada said less enthusiastically. 'I look forward to tasting that combo.'

'See you later.' Holly said brightly and went back to her room.

'Cheese and peanut butter?' Jada asked opening her sandwich to look inside.

'Well you were warned,' Sarah said stifling a smile. She walked up to her, stopping when she was stood between her legs. She kissed her hungrily, inhibited by the time they had before Holly came out of her room again.

'I don't know how long I can go on playing your *friend,*' Jada said.

'I know it's difficult,' Sarah said kissing her neck to which Jada let out a helpless sigh, 'I will tell her when I think she's ready.'

'And when will that be?' Jada asked still mesmerised by her touch.

'Soon... I promise,' she said. 'Are you coming to my room tonight? She asked nibbling her ear.

'Oh that depends,' Jada said huskily.

'On what?' Sarah asked tracing her neck with her

tongue

'On what's on offer...'

'Everything,' Sarah said seductively pulling her into another kiss, grateful to have such a special woman in her life.

'I don't know why you don't move in with us,' Sarah said to Jada as she loaded the dishwasher. 'You spend more time here than you do at your place.'

'Isn't that going to look a little strange to Holly?' Jada asked.

'Not anymore than it looks already.'

'Are you going to tell her about us?'

'No, not yet, she's only started to come to terms with Joe not being around, I don't want to confuse her.'

'Won't she feel betrayed when you do eventually tell her, it will be like we've been lying to her.'

'By the time I tell her, she will love you as much as I do, so it really won't matter.'

'If you say so,' Jada said unconvinced.

'Yes, I say so... so what do you say?'

'Okay,' she said after a short delay. 'No harm in trying, but, I will still be keeping my apartment, I'll rent it out when everything's settled.'

'Shall we collect your stuff tomorrow?' Sarah asked eagerly.

'Yes, okay,' she said, wondering if she was doing the right thing.

16

Emily switched off the TV and threw the remote control on the bedside table.

'That was lame,' she said sourly.

'I didn't think it was that bad,' Holly said.

'It was alright for a five year old,' she said. She couldn't understand what was wrong with her. Lately she had been feeling angry all the time. She had not told her mother because she didn't want to worry her.

'Do you miss your dad?' Holly asked Emily as they sat in the dark, the light from the streetlight shining in.

'I suppose,' she replied. 'Do you miss yours?'

'Loads,' she said. 'I love my mum and everything but I miss having my dad around he was so much fun.'

'Yeah I know what you mean,' Emily said. 'So why hasn't he been to see you since you've been back?'

'Dunno,' she said changing positions from her side onto her back. 'I overheard my mum talking to Jada about him coming to see me but he never did,' she said.

'How long has your mum been hanging around with Jada?' Emily enquired. 'They're always together, do you think they have a friendship like ours?' Emily asked innocently.

'Suppose, but they've got lots of money to do all adult stuff like go to casinos and eat in fancy restaurants.'

'Do they take you with them when they go to dinner?'

'Yeah, all the time but I prefer fish fingers to all that fancy stuff they eat; raw fish yuck,' she said pulling her face in the dark.

'I had that once,' Emily said trying to sound mature for age, what she omitted was the fact that she had thrown up straight away, raw tuna was a no-no for her.

'You're braver than me,' Holly said, 'you always have been.'

'Well I wouldn't go that far,' Emily said smiling to herself. She liked the fact that Holly looked up to her. When Sarah had taken Holly away with her years ago, Emily had been lost without her friend. She had not managed to find another friend like her and she was ecstatic that Holly was now back in her life and back at her school.

'Has... Has James had a girlfriend yet?' Holly asked tentatively.

'James,' Emily puffed, 'he doesn't even know what a girl is, all he understands is video games... boys are sooooo boring, and I don't know why everyone thinks they're so cool.'

'I think James is cool,' Holly blurted out.

'You can't fancy James,' Emily said with disdain in her voice. 'He's my brother and since you're like a sister to me that means he's like your brother too,' she said.

'But he's not my *real* brother though. I mean, if we got married we wouldn't go to jail or anything like that,' she said.

'Married!' Emily jerked up. 'To be married you have to be really old, and anyway like I said he's not into girls and he certainly wouldn't want to be your boyfriend, you'd be too young for him, everybody would laugh at him,' she said a little spitefully.

'Well, I didn't say I wanted him for a boyfriend anyway,' Holly retorted. 'I only said I thought he was cool.'

'What are you going on about boys for anyway?' Emily said. 'I'm your best friend and we only need each other.'

'I suppose,' Holly said thinking about James's smile.

'Do you know what I think we should do?' Emily said conspiratorially, jumping up on to her knees.

'What?' Holly asked equally excited.

'Go and see your dad at his office,' she said as if she had just invented the light bulb.

'And how are we going to do that?' Holly asked deflated. She lay back down.

'We bunk off school and catch the bus straight there, I know where my dad's office is,' she said thrilled by the secrecy of her plan.

'But we'll get into trouble,' Holly said.

'Oh stop being a baby, who's going to tell on us. I will tell my mum that your mum is picking us up from school and you can tell yours the same, no one will be any the wiser. James is going to his friend's house after school tomorrow so we wouldn't have to worry about him telling on us.'

'I don't know,' Holly said, uncertain.

'Do you want to see your dad or not?' she asked her, growing impatient. 'If I wanted to see my dad nothing would stop me,' she said lying back down and turning her back to Holly.

Neither friend spoke for a while.

'Emily?' Holly said gently. 'Are you awake?'

'Yes,' Emily answered her begrudgingly.

'Okay, we'll do it; we'll go to see my dad.'

Holly could not see the self-satisfied smile on Emily's face. She loved it when she got her own way.

***

'Hello little girls, are you lost?' Melanie, the receptionist at Withers and Peterson Solicitors asked the two schoolchildren who stood in the doorway of the office.

'No,' Emily said brashly, pushing Holly further in to the room. 'We're here to see Mr Withers,' she said with an air of confidence.

'Okay,' Melanie said a little patronising. 'You do know that this is a law office?'

'Yes,' she replied tartly, 'and did you know,' she said walking straight up to the desk, 'that *she*,' she turned to point at Holly who remained frozen to the spot, 'is his daughter?'

What a forceful little madam she is, Melanie thought about the little girl who stood confidently in front of her desk. When she was that age, she would have been scared to say "boo to a goose". *Children these days,* she inwardly sighed as she picked up the phone. 'Mr Withers - your daughter is in reception,' she said curtly. *First the ex wife, now a child... who would be next?* she thought. Joe had never mentioned any of this when he wined and dined her. She put the phone down, ignored the little brat in front of her, and spoke directly to the poor little girl who looked like a deer in headlights.

'Your father said go straight in,' she said kindly to her. Unlike the madam she was with, his daughter had obvious social issues.

'Thank you,' she said politely as Melanie showed them to her father's office.

'My... look at you,' Joe exclaimed when he saw Holly. He bent down and scooped her into his arms, hugging her for several seconds before putting her back onto the floor. 'Is your mother with you?' he asked looking behind her.

'No, just me.' Emily said before Holly could speak.

'Hello Emily,' Joe said briefly before turning his

attention back to his daughter. 'Haven't you grown, the last time I saw you were this high,' he said obviously exaggerating how small she was.

'No I wasn't,' she said shyly.

'Okay, how about this high,' he said raising his hand a bit higher.

She nodded. The whole scene repulsed Emily. She was embarrassed by the way Holly swooned over her father, *had she forgotten what he did to them*? she thought angrily.

'I'm glad you stopped by,' Joe said to Holly.

Liar, Emily thought, but knew better than to say anything.

'I was going to call you and arrange a day out, but we've been swamped with work,' he continued.

'It's okay,' she replied meekly.

'I know it's your birthday coming up next week, have you got any plans?'

She shook her head.

'Actually,' Emily stood forward. 'Holly is having a birthday party why don't you come as well?' she said sounding like a mature woman of thirty asking someone to a dinner party.

'I'd like that,' he said to Holly.

She nodded enthusiastically, 'so would I.'

'Good,' he said. 'That's settled.' He didn't mind having to sit through a boring children's party if it meant getting close to Sarah.

17

Raindrops patted tentatively on the window pane. Sitting alone in his apartment David reminisced about the trip he had just returned from. In China, he had cruised on the Yellow River, visited the Forbidden City and the Great Wall. His English speaking guide took him to see tombs in Xi'an, art museums, Buddhist temples and Mosques. He even cycled on top of the Xi'an city wall. He saw panda bears and to finish off he took a rickshaw tour of the Hutong district. From there he flew to Brazil and onto the Amazon where he went tree climbing and swam with pink dolphins. A smile spread across his face. He was content.

His thoughts turned to his family and a lump formed in his throat, his feeling of contentment vanished.

The intercom buzzed - interrupting his train of thought. He walked over and pressed the button and a moment later, his doorbell rang. Opening the door, he said, 'You're a sight for sore eyes.' He took her in his arms and held her tightly. 'I've missed you.'

'Me too.' He released her and she followed him into the apartment.

'So how did it all go?' she asked as she settled down on the sofa.

'Sally, it was a dream come true,' he gushed as he made his way to the kitchen and put the kettle on.

'I wish I could have been there to share it with you,' she called after him.

'It doesn't matter and if I'm honest I'm glad I went alone - no offence.'

'None taken,' she reassured him. 'How have you been? I thought you would have called at some point,' she said.

'I was so caught up in the moment I didn't give a

second thought to much else other than thoroughly enjoying myself,' he smiled as he walked back in with two steaming mugs of tea.

'You look tired,' she said to him.

'I suppose it's all the travelling, on top of everything else. So what's been going on in your world?' he asked as he placed the mugs on the coffee table.

'Up and down, mostly down but then it goes with the territory,' she said picking up her tea.

'Do you want to have dinner with me and the kids tonight? I'd love you to meet them.'

'If you think it would be okay,' she said, unsure. 'I don't want to ruffle anyone's feathers.'

'You could never do that,' he said looking at her fondly. He texted Laura a brief message asking if he could have the children over for dinner that evening. Within minutes, his phone bleeped with a message.

'I'll pick them up at five,' he said to Sally, as he read the message, 'if that's alright with you.'

'Yes, that's fine...'

'Is Chinese okay?'

'My favourite - but haven't you had enough of it?'

'No, never - I love it, I don't think the food over here will live up to the food I had in China though.' He smiled.

'No probably not. So where's your photo stash?' she asked looking around the room.

'You don't want me to bore you with them do you?' He laughed.

'Well I don't see myself going to any of those destinations anytime soon,' she said. 'So if you wouldn't mind I'd like to see them very much.'

'Okay,' he said sighing, 'but if it gets too boring you'll tell me, right?'

'Promise,' she said.

They spent the afternoon looking at David's holiday photos and when it was time, he left Sally in the flat and went to pick up James and Emily. Whilst he was gone, Sally set the table and found the menu for the Chinese delivery in one of the kitchen drawers.

***

David waited a few seconds before ringing the bell. It felt like a million butterflies were flying around in his stomach. He prayed the children were ready and he wouldn't have to go inside. Taking a deep breath, he pressed the bell and braced himself when he heard Laura coming to the door, whilst calling the children.

'They won't be long, do you want to come in and wait?'

He looked unsure.

'I don't bite you know,' she said injecting humour into the uncomfortable silence.

'Okay,' he said walking into the house.

'So how was your trip?' Laura asked trying to be civil.

'More than I could have expected,' he said his eyes lighting up.

'Good, I'm glad for you David.'

He glanced at the door anxious to leave.

'Am I that bad?' she asked him feeling hurt.

'What?' he asked her, confused by her comment.

'Is it that awful to spend any time in my company, you can't wait to get out of here.'

'No of course not,' he said. He couldn't bring himself to look into her eyes.

'David what went wrong?' she asked, despite her head telling her not to, her heart ached for an answer.

He ran his hand through his hair, 'I just did what I

felt I had to do,' he said truthfully.

'That's a pathetic excuse, you turned from a loving husband into a stranger in a matter of weeks, I don't recognise you anymore.'

'Do we really need to start all this again,' he said, 'the kids will be down in a minute and I don't want them to see us arguing.'

'We're not arguing David I just think I'm entitled to the truth,' she said.

'The truth...' he said letting out a small laugh.

'I'm glad you find this all so amusing,' she said sardonically.

'What is the point of dragging all this up again?' His mobile phone bleeped and he took it out of his pocket to read the message.

'You're seeing someone aren't you?' Laura challenged.

He turned away from her.

'Why can't you just admit it?' she pleaded. 'At least that way I can make some sense of why you are doing what you're doing to us.'

He sighed. 'Give it a break Laura... please,' he said with some exasperation, as James and Emily came into the room.

'Ready to go kids,' he said switching to the perfect parent persona. 'I'll drop them back about nine if that's okay,' he said to Laura as they all left the house.

***

Sally heard the children laughing in the hallway as the sound of David's key turned in the lock. She braced herself. It was not going to be easy.

'What did you buy me?' Emily was asking her father as they walked into the living room. She went quiet as soon as she saw Sally and eyed her suspiciously.

'Hey guys. I want you to meet my very good friend, Sally,' he said to them both as he ushered them towards her. He could feel their resistance as their bodies tensed.

'Hello,' Sally said in a friendly voice, 'your dad has told me so much about you.' They all felt the tension in the air.

'So why don't we order Chinese?' David said with an upbeat voice.

'I put the menu on the counter,' Sally said as David went over to pick it up.

'Great – right kids, what will you have?' he asked them handing James the menu. They were obviously very uncomfortable as neither of them had removed their jackets or attempted to sit down. It was like a standoff.

'Maybe I should go,' Sally said. 'I can come back later.'

'No, don't be silly, now let's order this takeaway,' David persisted. 'Take your jackets off and sit down, or don't you want your presents?' he asked. The children reluctantly took their jackets off and sat closely together on the sofa as David went to get the gifts from his bedroom.

'So your dad tells me you're a great football player,' she said to him, trying to break the ice. James smiled.

'He always tells everyone that,' he said bashfully.

'Well, it's true,' David said re-entering the room, carrying an armful of presents and placing them on the floor.

'Have you all decided what you want?'

'I'll have the one I normally share with Mum,' Emily said, her eyes darting towards Sally. Her intention did not go unnoticed and James nudged her in the side.

'What?' she said irritably.

'So you'll be having chicken chow mein then?' David said, winking at her.

'Yes,' she smirked.

'I'll order if you like,' Sally said once everyone had made their choice. She left the room and went to use the phone in the hallway.

'I have missed you guys so much,' David said sitting between them and hugging them both. He kissed them on the top of their heads. 'You know I love you both, don't you?' he said, choking with emotion.

'Aww Dad, don't start getting all slushy,' James said, feigning embarrassment. He was pleased to hear his father say those words – he'd been acting a bit distant lately. Something had changed in him and he couldn't understand what it was.

'There's nothing wrong with telling someone how much you love them, James,' David said seriously. 'That's the only thing that makes life worth living.'

'Like how you loved Mum once?' Emily said sarcastically. David turned to look at her.

'I will always love your mother,' he said to her seriously, 'always... sometimes things are too hard to explain. Even for adults,' he added sadly.

Sally had been waiting by the doorway not wanting to interrupt, but she did not want it to look like she was eavesdropping.

'It will be here in half an hour,' she said brightly.

'Great,' David said, 'so you can open your presents. Emily, yours are wrapped in yellow and James yours in...'

'Blue – there's only two colours, Dad!' James laughed.

'You've got a good eye for detail,' he said

jokingly. James and Emily squealed with delight as they unwrapped their presents and by the time they'd finished the Chinese had been delivered. They sat at the living room table eating whilst David told them about his trip and all the things he had done.

'Sounds awesome!' James said, excited. 'Will you take us with you next time, Dad?' he asked. David looked at Sally, who looked away.

'We'll see, son,' he said. 'So it's your big match on Saturday?'

'I knew you'd be back in time to come! Mum wasn't convinced,' he said, looking pleased with himself that he'd been right.

'I promised didn't I? I wouldn't miss it for the world.' James looked chuffed. 'And you, Madam, how are things going at school?'

'Alright I suppose... it's a bit boring sometimes.' David made a mental note to himself about talking to Laura about getting Emily moved up a year – she was academically gifted and her current level was obviously not stimulating enough.

'Can we play Scrabble?' she asked him.

'So you can beat me again?' he said, walking over to the sofa and retrieving the box from underneath.

'Sally, get prepared to be slaughtered by an eight year old,' David said looking at his daughter proudly.

18

'I was fucking right,' Laura said pacing back and forth in her living room.

'Can you make some tea please?' Sarah asked Jada as she tried to get Laura to sit down.

'You were right about what?'

'David *is* seeing someone – he introduced her to the kids this evening.'

'Are you sure?' Sarah asked, somewhat shocked by this revelation.

'Yes – my kids don't lie! Emily told me as soon as they got home,' she said, holding her head in her hands. Jada soon brought the tea in.

'Laura,' she said softly, 'drink this.' Laura looked up at her.

'I don't want that – I want a proper drink,' she said standing up, and then promptly sitting back down again. *No, she would not use alcohol as a crutch,* she reminded herself firmly. She picked up her tea instead.

'Thank you Jada,' she said smiling at her. 'Sorry for the outburst.'

'Don't worry about it.'

'Laura, listen to me – what exactly did Emily say?' Sarah asked.

'That his new girlfriend, *Sally*, was there when they got to his flat.'

'Did she actually say that she was his girlfriend?' Jada asked.

Laura tried to recall what Emily had told her.

'I can't remember what she said exactly, but if she's not his girlfriend, who is she then? David doesn't have female friends,' she snorted.

'I think you might be jumping the gun a bit, he's only just returned from holiday, if she was his girlfriend surely she would have gone with him?' Sarah tried to pacify her.

'There's nothing sure about David or had you forgotten – we're not dealing with a rational man anymore. Do you know I could never have imagined in a million years what you went through when Joe left you? Not even close to understanding. I thought I knew – I used to think to myself, *she's better off without him; she'll get over it...* God, if only I had known, I would have been a better friend.' She looked at Sarah glassy-eyed.

'Don't start putting yourself down Laura, you've always been there for me, nobody could have been more of a friend than you.'

'But I let you down! Why else would you have needed to leave your home, your work - everything, if I had been all you say I am?'

'I had my own path to walk Laura, and I needed to do it alone. For years, I used you, Joe, or a bottle of alcohol to prop me up. I was weak and I hated myself - my life was superficial. He threw everything money could buy at me, trying to fill that empty place in me, but it was never enough – nothing was big enough to fill my gaping hole. Joe leaving was the best thing that ever happened to me: I found me, the whole, undiluted me. It was hard Laura, but I did it because it was the only choice I had – I wasn't about to make Holly a motherless child, and that's what's got to be your inspiration – your children. How you deal with this is going to be a blueprint for them in their adult lives.' Laura sighed deeply.

'It's just the lies I can't deal with. I just wish he would just be straight with me so I know where I stand.' Laura played with the wedding ring on her finger; she still couldn't bring herself to remove it.

'Maybe that's the lesson you'll take away with you from all this,' Sarah said, sipping her tea.

'What's that then?'

'That people come and go in your life – nothing is stagnant, nothing can stay the same.'

'Oh god, if Dr Leigh could see me now,' Laura said dramatically.

'Laura, you're not Buddha, you're just a human being experiencing human experiences. Dr Leigh is fully aware that when we leave her office we have not been fixed – all she tries to give us is the tools to handle situations, it's not a test.'

'If it was, I would have failed big time,' Laura replied with a rueful smile. She inhaled deeply and concentrated on her breathing, totally blocking out the thoughts which were trying to break in. She was glad she was going to be seeing Dr Leigh in the morning – only her philosophies seemed able to talk her down from the edge.

***

'So how have you been coping?' Dr Leigh asked the following day.

'I wish I could say I was doing better. Well actually I am, or rather I was until yesterday,' she said.

'What happened yesterday?' Dr Leigh asked compassionately.

'I found out that my husband is having an affair and I blame myself. I think I overwhelmed him to the point where he couldn't take it anymore. I really tried to hold back the intensity of my feelings for him, and in hindsight, I guess I was always just waiting for him to tell me he'd had enough. From the beginning of our relationship I was feeling anxious to the point of feeling ill. I was always worried that he'd leave me like my father did...' She took a deep gulp of air. 'So maybe I subconsciously engineered the collapse of our relationship,' she finished, almost breathless.

'Did you have counselling when your father died?' Dr Leigh asked.

'No, I was only eight and my mother didn't believe in that sort of thing,' Laura said, feeling choked.

'How did that make you feel?' she asked.

'Like I didn't have a voice... that I didn't matter... maybe that's why I ended up being a people pleaser.'

'Maybe as a child you were powerless to have any impact on an adult's life, but as an adult you are not powerless.' Dr Leigh looked thoughtful and wrote in her notepad.

'I thought after my last session things were starting to click, but then it only took one thing to knock me down again, which proves I'm just weak,' she said, unable to look Dr Leigh in the eyes.

'It's not weakness Laura – it's fear. Think about it like this: fear is based on something that we think will happen in the future – it acts like a predictor. Yes, it can hit the bulls-eye sometimes – you fear your husband will leave you and he does, which then somehow justifies the fear in the first place, but once he leaves, you're scared how you're going to cope. Once you find you can cope then you fear you will never find another partner, and once you find another partner you fear he is going to leave you. Fear is always based on something that hasn't happened, yet we treat it as though it is real,' she explained patiently. 'In your case, the fear of losing possessions, like a loved one, comes back full circle to attachment, which is the key. Give David your full blessing to move on with his life and you will soon realise that he was never yours to lose...'

***

As Laura made her way home from the counselling session, she felt even more dazed than the first time she had met Dr. Leigh. Could she really do that - just move on, despite loving him as she did? She found herself taking a different route on the way home. Pressing a buzzer, she waited until she heard a click.

'David, it's Laura. I need to speak with you,' she said. Silence followed, and then the intercom buzzed.

'I'm on the ground floor,' he said. As she approached his door, a woman stepped out. Laura's heart caught in her mouth as she came face to face with the woman the children had been talking about. There was an awkward silence as the trio stood there.

'I'll be off then,' Sally said, feeling uncomfortable.

'Okay, I'll speak to you later,' David called after her. He pushed the door open for Laura to enter.

'Would you like a cup of tea?' he asked.

'Yes, please,' she said on the brink of tears. He'd barely looked at her. The man whom she had loved for the past ten years of her life was treating her as though she was a stranger.

'Take a seat and I'll bring it over,' he said, moving slowly to the kitchen.

'Do you mind if I open the blind?' she asked.

'I'd prefer it if you didn't,' he said, 'I've been getting these blinding migraines lately, the doctor suggested I sit in the dark, there's a lamp on the table you can put on.'

'It's alright, not if it's going to make you uncomfortable,' she said sitting down. He brought the tea to her and placed it before her.

'So how are you?' he asked as he sat down.

Better than you, she thought as she looked at him properly for the first time. He had lost a lot of weight and barely resembled the David she knew.

'I'm coping,' she said. 'You've lost a lot of weight.'

'Yeah, I know,' he grinned. 'I think I sort of went overboard with the dieting and exercise regime.'

'You think?' she asked incredulously.

'I have some protein shakes the doc prescribed for me. He said I'll bulk up in no time.'

'I hope so,' Laura said.   There was an uncomfortable silence. 'Was that her, then?' she asked.

'Who?' David asked absentmindedly.

'Forget it...' she said, 'it's none of my business who you see.'

'Laura, what...'

'Look.' She put her hand up to silence him. 'I didn't come here to talk about us, I came to find out what's happening about the kids for Christmas – what shall I tell them?' she asked, not looking at him.

'Laura, I don't know what's happening at the moment. It's best if they just think they're spending it with you.'

'Fine,' she said standing up. Her feeling of calm had now turned to resentment. 'At least we know where we stand.' She headed towards the front door. 'Don't get up, I'll see myself out,' she said sarcastically.

When he made no attempt to move she walked out the door and slammed it shut.

'Bastard,' she said as she got into her car and started it up. She noticed out of the corner of her eye that David was standing at the window of his apartment looking at her and stayed there until she drove off.

19

Despite not wanting a big deal made out of her party, Holly, under duress by Emily, had invited fifteen friends from school. The apartment had been decorated tastefully. Large silver balloons adorned the living room and caterers had been hired to prepare and make the food. Luckily, the apartment was big enough to hold all eighteen children and their parents. Holly looked every inch the birthday girl in her silver chiffon dress and sandals to match. Even James had paid her a compliment which had more than made her day. She still had not told Sarah she had invited her father. Emily told her it would be a nice surprise for her. The party was in full swing when the doorbell rang.

'We're not expecting anyone else,' Sarah said to Laura as she excused herself and went to open the door. She was taken aback when she saw Joe standing on the doorstep. He was dressed in a black leather jacket and faded jeans. He looked good and he knew it.

'Sarah...' he said smiling admiring her look; her chocolate coloured hair had been tousled into big brown curls, gently falling on her shoulders.

'Joe,' she said finding her voice, 'I wasn't expecting you.'

'Oh... didn't Holly tell you I was coming?' he said feigning disappointment. He knew she wouldn't tell Sarah that she had made her own way to see him.

'She must have done?' she lied. 'It must have just slipped my mind, come in,' she said opening the door further.

'Thanks,' he said. 'So where's the birthday girl?'

'Dad! You came!' she screamed, excitedly running up to him.

He hugged her and bent down on one knee. 'I told

you I would, didn't I,' he said. He was basking in the attention he was receiving from the mothers and children who had come out to the hallway to see who Holly was excited to see. He made sure that everyone was watching when he brought a velvet box out from inside his jacket. 'This is for the most precious girl in the world,' he said loud enough for the swooning mothers to hear.

'What is it Dad?' she asked excitedly.

'Why don't you open it and find out,' he said laughing. He turned to his audience and flashed them an infectious grin.

Holly opened the box and lined on the black velvet interior was a set of pearls. 'Oh Dad they're beautiful,' she said with tears in her eyes.

'Every princess deserves pearls,' he said, kissing her cheek and standing up. He soaked up the admiring glances from the women who still stood and openly stared at him.

'Come on Dad, come and see my birthday cake,' she said proudly taking his hand.

Although he had no interest in the cake he pretended he did for appearance's sake. 'Of course darling,' he said as he followed her.

What acting school did he drop out of? I've seen more convincing acting from five year olds, Jada thought shaking her head. She had his number straight away. The modelling world was full of slimy narcissistic men like him. She couldn't believe nobody else saw him for the fake he was. What had shocked her even more was the way that Sarah had reacted. She had been looking at him in awe.

She had never seen Holly look so happy, confident and alive. Since Jada had met her, she had been a subdued child only rarely showing glimpses of her true self. Yet with her father by her side, she glowed. She felt like crying, *the worst thing is she doesn't understand he's all for show.*

'So now you've seen the famous ex-husband,' Laura said to Jada handing her a glass of wine.

'Thank you. Yes so it seems.'

'At least Holly is happy,' Laura said thoughtfully.

For now, Jada felt like saying. How she wished she could be that naive.

'Jada, Jada,' Holly was heading towards her with her father in tow, 'meet my dad - Dad meet Jada, Mum's best friend.'

'Nice to meet you,' he said, charmingly drawn in by her beauty. Their eyes locked in a gaze. The normal reaction he got from women was missing. He felt a little deflated. She was by far the most attractive woman he had seen in a very long time and she hadn't shown the slightest bit of interest in him. *She must be a lesbian,* he thought, massaging his bruised ego.

'You have a wonderful daughter,' she said smiling down at Holly, not wanting to look at him for too long in case he guessed what she really thought of him.

'I remind myself of that every day,' he said.

'Look at the pearls my dad gave me for my birthday,' she chattered on.

Jada bent over. 'Wow, they are beautiful - just like you,' she said tapping the tip of her nose gently.

'I'm going to check on the food, please excuse me,' she said politely, desperately wanting to get away from him. The way she felt was not solely based on the fact he was her partners ex-husband, he just had a very dark aura that she couldn't stomach.

She found Sarah and Laura in the kitchen. 'Holly's having a wonderful birthday,' she said to them both.

'Yes she is,' Sarah said distracted.

'Is it possible to have a quick chat in private,' Jada asked her.

'Not at the moment - later,' she said as she walked off to her waiting guests.

'Is something wrong?' Jada asked Laura feeling slightly taken aback by Sarah's attitude. They had been together for a year and she had never seen this dismissive side to her before.

'I don't think so,' she said. 'Just the normal stresses of party hosting.'

Emily stood in the background whilst Holly had all the attention lavished on her. As she walked around the party, she caught snippets of the adults conversation. 'Isn't she lucky to have two gorgeous parents... Isn't she just adorable... Such a happy child.' She had also noticed that James was hanging around her like a sick puppy. She had never felt more invisible in her short life. She wished her dad was there because he always made her feel special *and now even he had someone new*, she thought, her mind conjuring up an image of Sally. She pulled the door to the toilet and was annoyed to find it locked. She was bursting to go. Then she remembered that her Aunt Sarah's bedroom had an ensuite. She let herself into her room and relieved herself. She was just about to flush the chain when she heard Sarah speaking to Jada. She gently set the toilet seat down and put her ear close to the door, praying that they wouldn't come in and find her.

'Is there any reason why you're avoiding me?' Jada asked Sarah.

'I'm not avoiding you, you are paranoid.'

'Don't play mind games with me Sarah,' she warned, 'you'll lose hands down every time.'

'Jada, I really don't know what you're talking about,' she said getting flustered.

'Look at the state you're in. What's happened to you in the space of a few hours?'

'Nothing's happened to me Jada. Now look I don't have time for this right now.'

'What's *this* then,' she asked.

'You and your accusations,' she said turning on her. 'We aren't married...' she blurted out. 'You've no right to make any kind of demands from me.'

'Whoa - ' Jada held up her hands, '- where did that come from....'

'Look we'll talk later,' she said half apologising. 'Someone might hear us.'

'So you do know what it is,' she said sitting on the bed, fully aware that Sarah knew how she had been treating her.

'What?' Sarah said somewhat oblivious.

'I accepted you in my life completely heartedly, I introduced you as my lover to my friends, my family everyone.'

Emily put her hand to her mouth. *She's gay! Aunt Sarah is gay and so is Jada. So much for a perfect family*, she thought with glee.

'... and this is how you repay me - by putting a bunch of strangers before me, before us. I thought you were different Sarah. I really fell for your bullshit didn't I, live and let live, what a pile of crap.'

'Can you keep your voice down,' Sarah said panicking.

'I'll do better than that,' she said collecting her coat from the cupboard.

'Where are you going?' she said.

'Away from you and this bullshit,' she said.

Sarah grabbed her arm. 'Please - Jada just wait.'

Jada shrugged her arm off her. 'No Sarah, I think I've waited long enough, don't you?' she said meeting her eyes. Sarah said nothing as Jada walked out.

Moments later Emily heard the bedroom door close for a second time. Convinced that the room was empty, she hurried from the ensuite and back into the living room. She felt a lot better now that the shine had come off Holly's halo.

'Where's Jada?' Laura asked Sarah as the remaining guests left.

'She had an appointment to keep,' she lied.

'Sarah, it's me you're talking to, I know when you're lying.'

'Alright, we had an argument,' she finally admitted.

'Nothing serious I hope,' Laura said. 'I really like Jada and you two make a great couple. You're lucky to have found someone who genuinely loves you, warts and all,' she said squeezing her shoulder.

Sarah's eyes were brimming with tears. 'You had true love with David,' she said.

'Yeah right, that's why I'm here alone because he's so madly in love with me,' she said sarcastically. 'Anyway what did you two row about?'

'She thought I was embarrassed about our relationship.'

Laura was shocked. 'I can't believe she thought that, you two are so natural together.'

'I'm ashamed to admit that she may have been right. I didn't exactly tell anyone here tonight who she was. And you know I haven't told Holly yet.'

'You are kidding me right, you care what those two-faced fuckers think about you. Oh Sarah I thought you had gotten over that "caring what people think about you" bullshit. And it's about time you told Holly, you have been lying to her long enough,' Laura was angry. The very thought that Sarah had treated Jada that way sickened her. She deserved better.

The conversation was cut short when James and

Emily said they were tired and wanted to go home. It had been a long day for everyone.

'I'll see you tomorrow,' Laura said to Sarah, her displeasure evident.

'See you then,' she said sheepishly. She put her head against the door.

'You never used to get so stressed giving parties,' Joe said.

'You're still here?' she said.

'Yes, I wanted to talk to you.'

'Can it wait, I'm really tired.'

'It won't take long.'

'Okay, you can talk while I load the dishwasher.'

He followed her into the kitchen. Holly, who had seen them enter, followed and for the second time that evening Sarah was eavesdropped on.

'Those pearls were a bit extravagant weren't they?' she said.

'Do you think so? Holly loved them.'

'And where exactly is she going to wear them? To school? Something more age appropriate would have been fine.'

'Look - the most important thing is that the party went really well,' Joe said. 'Holly really seemed happy.'

'I think that was more to do with you being here than her party...'

'We make a great team,' he said coming up behind her. 'I made a big mistake when I left you,' he said. 'I want to try again,' he continued. 'I want us to be a family again.'

Holly's heart was in her mouth as she waited to hear her mother's reply. They were going to be a family again. Just at that moment, she heard the key rattling in the door. It was Jada. Holly ran to the door before Jada could enter.

'Hey what's the matter?' she said bumping into Holly.

'Don't go in there Jada,' Holly said in a whisper. 'Dad's making up with Mum and we're going to be a family again.' Holly's face beamed with joy.

Jada looked into the girls innocent eyes. She knelt down beside her, and in a hushed voice said,

'It's ok Holly I won't go in there darling. I'll let you have your dream come true. But you have to do me a favour.'

'Anything,' Holly said with unbearable excitement.

'Don't tell your mum I came back okay.'

Holly nodded.

'Do you promise?'

'Yes, I promise.'

'Happy birthday Holly,' Jada said as she turned around and walked away.

20

'Quieten down please,' Mrs Bush, the schools art teacher said in a raised voice. 'Johnny sit down and stop doing that,' she said to a little brown haired boy who was pulling the pigtails of the girl who sat in front. Mrs Bush was a small round woman with her black hair pulled tightly into a bun at the back of her head. Her features were soft and her eyes kind.

'Today we are going to be doing family portraits, now I want you to go in two's and collect the paper and pens from the art cupboard. We'll start off from this table and move upwards; Polly and Sam you go first.'

The children obediently rose from their desk and gathered the material needed from the art cupboard.

'Who are you going to paint?' Holly asked Emily when they sat back at their desks after their turn.

'I've got an idea, why don't you paint my family and I'll paint yours, it's silly trying to paint ourselves,' she said.

'Okay Emily, I'll make you look really pretty,' she said looking at her best friend like a puppy.

Emily smiled sweetly. 'Thanks,' and started drawing.

When the class had finished, Holly showed Emily her final product, a picture of David, Laura, James and Emily sat together smiling. Emily was impressed.

'That's a good try,' she said.

'Can I see yours?' Holly asked trying to take a peek.

'No, not yet, wait until I show the whole class, I think you'll like it,' Emily said.

Mrs Bush called each of the children to the front of the class to present their work. Emily was the last to be called.

'Right Emily, would you like to tell us about the people in your portrait,' she said sitting down on her seat.

'Yes, I've drawn a portrait of Holly's family.' She turned her picture towards the class showing the three figures. 'This is Holly, she said pointing to the little figure with two bunched pig tails, this is her mum Sarah and this...' she stopped dramatically and looked at Holly, '...is Jada, Holly's mum's girlfriend'. She swirled around from her left side to her right so each of the pupils could see.

Holly stood up and glared at Emily. 'No it isn't why are you saying that! She's my mum's friend!' she cried.

'She's her girlfriend, I heard her say it with my own ears,' Emily said smugly as she returned to her seat.

She looked over at Holly who had sat back down, and was covering her face with her hands, trying to block out the sniggering from the other children.

Mrs Bush looked stunned and for a few seconds she couldn't speak.

'Quiet please,' she said clapping her hands together in a short succession

The sniggering and nudging of the next person continued. 'I said quiet,' she said, raising her voice. 'The next person I hear a sound from will be explaining to the headmaster exactly what they find funny. Emily, that was not a very nice thing to do to your friend, I want to talk to you after class,' she said seriously.

'but Miss - ' Emily whined.

'- I don't want to hear another word.'

The school bell broke the silence. The children rose quickly in an effort to go and spread the gossip. Mrs Bush thought to herself sadly, *children can be so cruel.* She sighed, she was grateful she had decided to be childfree.

'Holly can you also stay behind please,' she said gently.

'Emily you wait outside until I come and get you.' Emily stood up and joined a bunch of sniggering girls as they all left the classroom.

Mrs Bush took a seat beside Holly, who was crying quietly now. She did not know what to do about comforting the weeping child. She thought maybe it was best that she asked her mother to come and collect her. It was unfortunate that the situation had to be dealt with this way, it was as though Holly were being punished but she'd prefer her to go home rather than be taunted all day. And for such a malicious act to come from Emily, *who would have thought it?*

'Let's go to see the headmaster,' she said taking her limp hand. She left Holly sitting outside while she went in to talk to the headmaster.

'What can I do for you?' he asked.

'I had an incident in class today... Emily Peterson, how can I put it - well she... sort of outed Holly's mum as a lesbian to the whole class.'

'I see...' he said thoughtfully. 'We've been having a few problems with Emily's brother fighting, apparently the father has moved out and these problems seem to be stemming from that.'

'I thought maybe it would be best to send Holly home today, she is very upset and I don't want her to be taunted for the rest of the day.'

'Ok, I will call Holly's mum to come and get her. Can you also send Emily to me so I can speak to her; I think it's best we also inform her mother.'

Mrs Bush left the office and walked back to the classroom. Emily was still stood outside the door.

'The headmaster wants to see you, so go there now,' she said sternly.

Tears began to stream down Emily's face as she walked down the corridor to the headmaster's office and knocked on his door.

'Come in.'

Emily opened the door and sat down, Mr Picard handed her a tissue.

'That was a very vindictive and hurtful thing you did to Holly today,' he said to her with a hint of anger in his voice. 'Can you explain to me why you did it?'

'I don't know why, I just thought everyone should know,' she whined.

'No, you did it to humiliate your friend in front of everyone; there was no reason to tell anyone in that manner, you could have spoken to Holly about it privately. Anyway, I have called your mother and she will be coming to see me this afternoon. You can go out to play now, and I do not want to hear that you have been discussing this further with anyone, do I make myself clear?'

'Yes sir,' she said barely audibly.

Half an hour later there was a firm knock on the door. Mr Picard opened it to find Holly's mum standing there, concern on her face.

'Please come in,' he said.

Sarah stepped into his office to see Holly looking small and dishevelled sitting in a chair that was bigger than she was. She dropped her bag on the floor and went to her, kneeling beside her. She took her hand in hers. 'Are you okay my baby?' she said, her voice shaking with emotion.

Holly nodded weakly.

'Come on,' she said softly, 'let's get you home.' She stood up and faced Mrs Bush who had come to join them.

'I'm terribly sorry this happened this way, I had no way of stopping it, the class were only drawing family portraits,' she said with guilt written across her face.

'It's not your fault,' Sarah said sincerely as she took Holly's hand. 'Thank you for looking after her,' she said as they left the office.

As they approached the entrance, James ran speedily towards them. 'Holly!' he shouted. They both turned and waited for him. He was breathless when he reached them.

'Hello Aunt Sarah,' he said to Sarah first, then he looked at Holly, sorrow in his eyes. 'I'm sorry Emily did that to you,' he said.

She raised her eyes to meet his. 'That's okay.'

'No - it's not,' he said, 'it was a cruel thing to do and a lot of people think so too.'

'They do?' she said looking hopeful.

'Yes,' he said reassuringly. 'When you come to school tomorrow, I'll walk you to your class, if anyone has anything to say, they can say it to me first,' he said gallantly.

Sarah leant over and kissed the top of his head. 'Thanks James,' she said.

'That's alright,' he said blushing. 'See you tomorrow then Holly,' he said before running off to his next class.

Sarah was pleased to see the colour had come back into Holly's pale skin. They drove home in silence after Holly insisted she didn't want to talk about what happened. Sarah felt sick to her stomach that she had been the cause of her child's humiliation. She thought about what Joe had said the evening before, about them making a go of it again as a family - a normal family, where they could all fit in. She looked at Holly and

knew she had to make a decision, and *fast*.
***

When they got home, Holly went to her room and shut the door. Sarah made herself a coffee. *How do I approach this*, she thought to herself. She set her cup down on the worktop and walked to Holly's door. She gave a gentle tap and then opened it slowly.

'Can we talk?' she asked standing at the doorway.

Holly nodded and put her pen down and looked at her suspiciously.

Sarah walked in and sat on the floor by the bed.

'Things are pretty confusing at the moment, aren't they? I don't think I've been honest enough with you about Jada and my feelings for her.' Even though she had played these words repeatedly in her mind, she felt strange actually saying them, admitting them to her daughter. 'Maybe if I had been more open with you, what happened at school could have been avoided.' She paused, frightened to go on. She took a deep breath. 'It's true that Jada is... well was my girl... partner and I love her very much,' she continued when Holly didn't turn away from her in disgust, 'and despite what other people say, there is nothing wrong with loving someone who is the same sex as you. That's what's so great about love Holly, you can love many things.'

'Why did you lie to me?' Holly interrupted.

'I didn't tell you about Jada because I knew how much you were upset about your dad and I needed you to know that you are my top priority and nothing will ever change that.'

'So Dad isn't going to be living with us again?'

Sarah moved up onto the bed and took Holly's hand. 'No he isn't, if I could love him as much as I love Jada I would stay with him forever, but I don't, and he doesn't love me like that. I know how much it would mean to you for us all to be together again but it wouldn't work.'

'So is Jada coming back?'

'I don't know.'

'Is it because I asked her to stay away?'

Sarah was shocked but tried to mask it. 'When did you ask her to stay away?' she asked evenly.

'The night of my birthday, you were talking to Dad in the kitchen and Jada came home. I told her not to interrupt you because you and Dad were getting back together,' she said looking down in shame.

Sarah's heart was pounding, Jada *had* come back. Now she understood why she hadn't returned any of her calls. She was at a loss what to do.

'I'm sorry Mum.'

'Hey,' she said wrapping her arms around her, 'you've got nothing to be sorry for,' she kissed the top of her head. 'Do you have any questions you'd like to ask me?'

Holly shook her head.

'If you ever want to ask me anything...'

'I know,' Holly said.

'Shall we stay in tonight or do you fancy going round to Aunt Laura's, you don't have to see Emily, I'm sure James would be more than happy to entertain you.'

At that, Holly's eyes lit up. 'Aunt Laura's,' she said brightly.

Sarah laughed. Young love, it was so innocent.

***

Laura cried. Her heart was broken. She could not believe a child of hers could act so horribly. The scene replayed repeatedly in her mind as she imagined Holly sitting there whilst her best friend betrayed her in front of the whole class. For the first time since Emily was born, she could not bear to look at her. She was ashamed to admit, mother or not, that the small child's behaviour repulsed her. She knew that both children were having a hard time coping with David leaving home, but that did not validate what Emily did to Holly. When she had picked Emily up to go to the headmaster's office, Emily had acted as though nothing was wrong. She admitted quite openly what she had done in class and had no remorse.

Hearing the doorbell ring, Laura wiped the tears away from her eyes, there was nothing she could do about them being swollen. As soon as she saw Holly standing next to Sarah she knelt down and held her. 'I'm so sorry,' she said fighting to keep the tears from falling.

'It's alright Auntie Laura,' she said hugging her back.

Laura looked up at Sarah. There was no need for words, their look said it all, *how did we ever get into this mess?*

'Hey Holly,' James said, 'wanna watch me play my new game?' he asked.

Holly looked up at her mother and Sarah nodded with a smile.

The two women made their way into the living room and sat side by side on the sofa.

'I'm still in shock about Emily's behaviour,' Laura said. 'When Mr Picard was explaining what happened I kept thinking he must be talking about another child.'

'Maybe you should get her some counselling,' she said.

'That might not be a bad idea, what with James fighting, Emily bullying, god knows what will happen next.'

'Have you spoken to Emily about it yet?' she

asked.

'Only briefly, I was so angry I just wanted her out of my sight,' she admitted. 'If I'm honest with you, I don't think now is the best time for me to talk to her, I may say something I'll regret.'

'Yeah maybe it's best you wait a while,' Sarah agreed.

'She said she heard you and Jada arguing at Holly's party.'

Sarah looked anguished. 'Oh right, so that's how she knew. I've just had the dreaded talk with Holly, she took it quite well, considering the day she's had.'

'Children are a lot stronger than we give them credit for. Have you heard from Jada?'

'Nope and I don't think I will. Holly told Jada I was getting back with Joe,' she said.

'Are you kidding?' Laura asked shocked.

'I wish I was,' she said sadly.

'I'm so sorry.'

'It would have helped had Jada explained before running off.'

'I'm really surprised that you reacted the way you did at that party though, you never used to care what people thought about you,' Laura said.

'That was before I had a kid, what happened to Holly was exactly what I was trying to avoid. Looks like it was all in vain, everyone will know now, I'm sure it was the talk of the school run today.'

'Who bloody cares,' Laura said emphatically.

Sarah sighed. 'I really do love her, everything just happened naturally with Jada, I could just be myself.'

'Do you think women are your thing now.'

'Who knows,' Sarah said. 'Women, men, it all ends the bloody same... in heartbreak... at least when it comes to me it does.'

'I know the feeling,' Laura said mournfully. 'I keep wondering whether it was really necessary for David to leave his family to try and capture his dreams.'

'I don't know Laura, everyone has their own reasons, we might not understand why people do the things they do.'

'At the rate we're going, we'll both end up as two old maids,' she said trying to lighten the mood.

'That'll be right,' Sarah said.

'Stay for dinner, it's nearly ready and there is no use us both being alone,' she said.

'Okay, I forgot to tell you what Joe suggested last night...' she said as they walked into the kitchen.

'Oh god I dread to think,' Laura said opening a bottle of wine and pouring two glasses.

'He had the gall to suggest we get back together.'

Laura pulled a face in disbelief. 'You are joking aren't you?'

'Nope, he said we should do it for Holly's sake.'

'I hope you told him where to stick it,' Laura said looking at her friend intently.

'Obviously,' Sarah said. 'He'd guessed about me and Jada, most probably because she didn't swoon under his gaze, he said he found the idea of me being with her quite sexy.'

'That man has no shame.'

'He never has had, at least he's agreed to see Holly at the weekends, so that's something I suppose.'

'Let's see how long he keeps it up for. Can you pass me the pasta out the cupboard please.'

'Sure,' Sarah said as she retrieved the pasta and handed it to Laura.

'You're sauce smells great,' she said leaning over the pan.

'Taste it and tell me if it needs more salt,' Laura

said handing her a spoon.

Sarah took a spoonful of the red bubbling sauce and blew on it before putting it in her mouth. 'Beautiful,' she said smiling at Laura .

'Good, it shouldn't be long now.'

'Do you think I should talk to Emily before dinner?'

'If you think it will do any good,' Laura said.

'I can only try,' she said as she went up to Emily's room. She knocked softly on the door to which there was no reply. She turned the handle and walked in to find Emily curled up in a foetal position on her bed rocking from side to side. She was sobbing quietly. Sarah hurried over to her and gathered her in her arms.

'Emily,' she said,

'I'm sorry, I'm sorry,' she kept repeating.

'Hey shh shh,' Sarah said comforting her.

'I... didn't... mean ... it,' she sobbed. 'I... didn't mean any harm.'

'I know you didn't baby,' Sarah said still rocking her.

Holly appeared at the door. Her face full of compassion. 'Is she okay?' she asked Sarah.

'She'll be fine,' she said.

'I'm sorry Holly,' she said through blurred tears. 'I'll make it better tomorrow.'

'Come and sit with Emily,' Sarah said to Holly. 'I think she needs a friend more than anything right now.'

She left the two girls alone, Holly comforting her whilst she apologised profusely to her.

'I do think Emily needs to speak to someone,' Sarah said as she entered the kitchen.

'What did she say?'

'That she's sorry. She's in a bit of a state, Holly is sitting with her.'

'Well at least she now has the decency to admit she's done something wrong.'

'I just think she's hurting Laura, her whole world has come crashing down around her and she's just trying to make sense of it.'

'That's all very well, but she is still accountable for her behaviour today. I can't just gloss over it Sarah. I don't want her to grow up thinking it's alright to step on people just because she's unhappy with her life.'

'Let's just hope she has learnt a lesson today.'

'Yes indeed.'

The following morning Laura asked Mrs Bush if Emily could say something to the class about picking on people because they are different. Laura had spoken to Emily at length about what she had done and the consequences of her actions. Emily had been very tearful and Laura believed her when she said she really regretted her actions.

'Yesterday I did a horrible thing to my best friend Holly. I told you all something that I shouldn't have. Not because Holly's mum having a girlfriend is wrong, but for the reason I did it. I was unhappy so I didn't want her to be happy either. Telling other people's secrets and name calling hurts and I'm sorry that I behaved like that and I'm sorry that I was so horrible to my best friend.'

21

Laura opened the door looking flushed. For one split second, Joe wondered if that's what she looked like just after lovemaking. 'Here's my little munchkin,' he said bringing his attention back to Laura admiring her look as always.

'Hello Holly,' Laura said bending down to kiss the top of her head. 'Run along - Emily and James are waiting for you.'

She spun round and cuddled Joe. 'See you later Dad,' she beamed. Casually dressed in blue jeans and a black shirt he looked the perfect poster boy.

'I've never seen Holly looking happier,' Laura said. Sarah had called her and asked if she could watch Holly for a few hours if Joe dropped her off. Sarah was going to London to see if Jada was at her apartment, as she still hadn't returned any of her calls.

'It looks that way doesn't it,' he smiled drinking in her appearance. There was an awkward silence. 'How have you been Laura?' he asked, 'I wanted to come by ages ago and offer a shoulder to cry on but I'm probably the last person on earth you'd want to lean on.'

'I'm getting through it,' she said ignoring his last remark.

'And the kids?'

'Oh they're tough little cookies. David still sees them so it's not as bad as it could be -' she said, '- oh I didn't mean...'

He held his hand up to silence her. 'No offence taken. I know what mistakes I've made.'

They were interrupted when Emily ran up to her mother pulling her hand. 'Mum we're ready to eat now.'

'Okay Emily - but don't be rude I'm in the middle of talking to Holly's dad, say hello.'

'Hello Mr Withers,' she said reluctantly.

'Hello Emily,' he said stepping forward towards her but she backed away. He looked up at Laura. 'What time shall I pick Holly up?'

'About nine?'

'Sounds good,' he leant towards her and kissed her cheek, inhaling the sweet scent of her perfume. 'Good to see you again,' he said softly in her ear before turning around and walking down the path. Laura looked after him. He had seemed like the old Joe she had known. Sincere and caring. And Holly was obviously over the moon that her dad was back in her life. She closed the door and followed Emily into the kitchen.

'Auntie Laura may I use the telephone please?' Holly asked.

'Of course you can darling, use the phone in the hall,' she said as she began gathering the ingredients for dinner. Holly took the phone off the receiver and began dialling the mobile number she read from the scrap paper she was holding. It went straight to voicemail. She spoke quietly as she left a message. 'Please come home Jada.'

***

The end of the evening could not have come any sooner for Laura. As much as she had enjoyed spending time with the children, she was knackered. She was looking forward to relaxing in a long hot bath. She had called Sarah to ask if Holly could stay overnight and she had agreed. She said she would call Joe and tell him not to bother picking her up later that evening. She got the children settled into bed then ran herself a bath with scented bath salts. Half an hour later her whole body and mind felt revived. Wrapping herself up in her thick cotton nightgown, she was dismayed when she heard the bell ring. *Who could that be*? She thought, thinking it might be David.

She didn't have time to change, so she answered the door in her gown. It was Joe.

'I'm sorry I'm a bit late, got caught in traffic,' he said apologetically.

'Oh Joe. I'm afraid it's been a wasted journey, Sarah said she was going to call you to let you know Holly was going to be staying over the night,' she said tightening the cord on her nightgown.

'Damn,' he said, 'my battery is dead, she most probably left me a message.' He eyed her in the evening light. 'Do you mind if I use your loo quickly, I'm bursting,' he said innocently.

'Er...no...of course not,' she said opening the door wide enough so he could enter.

'Thanks,' he said as he rushed past her.

She shut the door and went into the kitchen. She heard the toilet flush and heard Joe coming down the stairs. He was in the kitchen before she managed to meet him at the bottom of the stairs.

'Blimey, it looks like you've been cooking a banquet,' he said eyeing the empty pots and pans strewn over the worktop.

Laura smiled. 'I know - I just don't have the energy to deal with it all tonight.'

'I'll give you a hand,' he said taking off his jacket, despite protests from Laura. 'Pour yourself a drink and I'll get stuck in,' he said as he began to collect the children's cups from the kitchen table.

Laura went to the fridge and poured herself a glass of wine. 'Would you like a glass?' she asked Joe.

'Oh go on then, you've twisted my arm, I'll have whatever you're having.'

She passed him a glass.

'Thanks,' he said accepting it from her and taking a quick sip. 'Ahh just what the doctor ordered.' He placed the glass on the table and began loading the dishwasher.

Laura sat down on the stool. 'I feel guilty not helping,' she said.

'Don't be silly - this is nothing compared to cooking, give me the clean up job any day,' he said, stopping what he was doing for a brief moment to look at her. 'You know I really admire the way you have handled things. I know things could not have been easy for you when David left but look at you,' he said in a tone of admiration.

'Don't,' she said bashfully, 'I have to carry on for my kids sake - and my own sanity,' she said quietly, she lowered her head, fighting the urge to cry. She tried to bring herself back to the present moment, just like Dr Leigh had advised her whenever she started to feel melancholy or was longing for the past or future. Surprisingly, it had actually worked but sometimes the thoughts caught her unaware and she couldn't help herself at that moment in time. She took a deep breath and began to concentrate on her breathing. Joe was beside her in a second, kneeling down next to her.

'David is a bloody idiot,' he said, 'leaving someone like you, I don't know what's got in his head,' he put his hand over hers. 'I'm always here for you if you ever need to talk,' he said softly.

'Thanks Joe,' she said feeling uncomfortable at his closeness. 'I think I'll help you clean up,' she said standing up. 'I'll just go and get some decent clothes on.'

'You look beautiful as you are,' he said.

'Of course I do. I think that drink has gone straight to your head,' she said as she left the living room and went to her bedroom. She pulled on jeans, and a baggy jumper, then pulled her hair back into a ponytail. She returned down stairs and was pleased to see that in the ten minutes she had been gone, Joe had made great in roads with the cleaning of the room.

'Wow, I'm impressed,' she said genuinely.

'I'm more than just a pretty face,' he said. 'All that's left to do is wipe down the surfaces. I've put all the rubbish out front,' he responded gallantly.

'I can't thank you enough Joe,' Laura said going over to him and kissing him on the cheek. As she moved backwards, he pulled her closer again.

'Yes you can,' he said as he thrust his face towards her attempting to kiss her on the mouth. She pulled away from him hard.

'Joe! Are you crazy. What are you doing?' she asked.

'What I've wanted to do from the first moment I ever laid eyes on you,' he asserted, brazening it out now that he had said what was on his mind. He moved towards her.

'Joe!' she snapped trying to bring him back to his senses. 'I think you'd better leave,' she said walking towards the door.

'Laura, we aren't doing any harm,' he said following her. She had already reached the front door and was holding it open.

'Just leave Joe,' she said as he tried to say something to her. 'I can't believe you'd try and pull that shit with me - I'm a married woman,' she said aghast.

He stopped before he went through the door. 'I can't see a husband around here,' he said nastily. 'Can you?' he said with a humourless smile.

The concerned friend he had been portraying only half an hour ago was gone now. 'I thought you were

David's friend,' she cried glaring into his face. 'You're a right bastard,' she said, a tremor in her voice.

His face was impassive. 'Yeah and you're a frigid bitch, no wonder he left you,' he spat and slammed the door behind him leaving Laura in a state of shock.

What was going on? she thought looking aimlessly at the back of the door as though Joe was still standing there. *Has everyone gone mad?* She double locked the door, feeling unsafe for the first time ever. She didn't think he would return but, then again, she never thought that he would come on to her. She felt sick to the stomach. What kind of leech had been living amongst them all those years? She felt isolated. She had no one to talk to about what had just happened. She couldn't speak to Sarah about it. She didn't want to jeopardise Holly's relationship with her father when she just had it back. She couldn't even tell David. The temporary blanket that she had been covered with all her life was truly gone. She was shocked when she realised that she didn't care.

She called Sarah. For the first time in her life, she felt light and free. She wasn't going to burden her friend with what happened with Joe. She realised it wasn't personal, he would hit on anything with a pulse. She didn't need anyone to protect her anymore. She would call him in the morning and put him straight about a few things. After a few rings, she answered.

'Did you see her?' she asked Sarah.

'No, she wasn't there.'

'Did you leave a note?'

'Yes I left her a letter explaining everything,' she said. 'Hold on a minute let me get my keys out, I've just arrived home.'

Laura could hear the rustling of her bag then the rattling from the keys as she put one in the door.

'She'll come back when she reads it,' Laura was saying to a shell shocked Sarah.

'She doesn't need to, I can tell her in person,' she said as she looked at Jada standing in the hallway.

22

'Whoa, what's going on here?' Sarah said as she moved out the way of a big bearded man carrying a large office chair out from Laura's house. 'Is there something you're not telling us?' she teased.

'And I thought it was only us that kept secrets,' Jada chimed in.

'Come in you two,' Laura laughed, waving them both in, 'before the neighbours hear you, they'll start thinking I'm a wanton woman.'

The three women went through to the Living room.

'So what's all this about then?' Sarah asked.

'I'm moving on, getting rid of the rest of David's stuff and redecorating,' Laura said brightly. 'I don't know why but I don't think he is ever coming back, so there's no point me sitting around moping anymore.'

Sarah cut in. 'That's great, I'm glad to hear it.'

'When I saw him the other day I just felt sorry for him, he's lost weight and he looks about ninety. So he must have a conscience about leaving us after all. For a minute I was happy to see him looking so bloody miserable holed up in that flat, but you know what, I actually feel sorry for him, it's his loss.'

'Laura you know I would never get involved in your relationship with David, I respect you both so much, but I think you should give him a bit of slack, I'm sure he's hurting as well.'

'Yeah of course he is, is that why he said the kids should stay with me for Christmas, doesn't sound like the doting father to me. I am through, I feel strong enough to cut the cord now and let him get on with his life while I get on with mine,' she said jubilantly. 'For the first time I feel like me, not David's wife, not a mother but me, Laura.'

'Good for you,' Jada said. 'If it wasn't so early I'd pop open a bottle of bubbly.'

'I'm sure one glass wouldn't do any harm,' Laura said. 'I have a bottle of champagne in the fridge, we can have a bucks fizz, I have freshly squeezed orange juice as well.'

'I don't need telling twice,' Jada said as she went to the kitchen to prepare the drinks.

'Do you really think you're stronger now?' Sarah asked her.

'Definitely! Had you asked me that question a few months ago I would have thought it was impossible, I don't know how to explain it but I feel like a new me, I'm changing all the bedding to the colours I like and rearranging the furniture. David said he doesn't want his desk and cupboards so they are going to the dump today.'

'I'm really proud of you do you know that?' Sarah said.

'Isn't it funny how you're always there when I need you the most.'

'That's what friends are for Laura, the good and the bad.'

Jada came back with the drinks. Each of the women took a glass.

'I'd like to make a toast,' Laura said holding her glass in mid air. 'To the future and to good times,' she said. Whilst she drank, she failed to notice the other two women did not seem to share her enthusiasm

23

Sally was woken by the sound of her mobile phone vibrating on her bedside table. The figure sleeping next to her stirred and groaned.

'What time is it?' he asked.

'2.30a.m.,' she said, looking at the time on her mobile before answering it. 'Yes, this is Sally Bernard,' she said to the caller. What the person relayed to her sent chills down her spine. She jerked up in bed and fumbled to switch the bedside lamp on. 'Thank you,' she said her voice fraught with emotion. She immediately rang off and started to dial a number she read out from her address book.

'Now who you calling?' her sleeping companion asked, irritated. Sally ignored him and pressed the buttons then waited for someone to answer. Finally, a tired voice answered.

'Hello?'

'Laura, this is Sally. I think it's time that we met.'

***

David woke up sweating, the pain in his heart making him feel breathless. Laura lay beside him sleeping peacefully so he eased his way out of the bed and walked as quietly as he could to the bathroom. He switched on the light, squinting as he tried to block it out. The pain was getting worse – he was more convinced than ever he had an ulcer. Damn all that gourmet food and drink I've been consuming lately. It had obviously played havoc with his system and now he was paying for it. Change of diet from tomorrow, he thought, standing up and looking at himself in the mirror. It had never been this bad before – another shot passed through his intestines. He took a deep breath, holding onto the side of the bath. Within a few seconds, the pain had started to ease but his forehead glistened with sweat and his eyes looked dull. He bent his head over the sink and splashed several handfuls of cold water onto his face. It made him feel a bit better and he patted his face dry before heading back to bed.

The next morning he phoned and booked an appointment for a check-up. If he did have an ulcer, the doctor would at least be able to give him something to ease the pain. As he walked into the kitchen, his favourite song was playing on the radio and James and Emily sat sullenly on their chairs waiting for their breakfast.

'Cheer up you two,' he said playfully ruffling their hair, 'this is what happens when you don't go to bed early,' he said mockingly. Neither child looked amused. He'd heard them through the bedroom wall the previous night talking in hushed voices.

'Good morning, gorgeous,' he said to Laura as he spun her round to dance with him.

'Good morning to you too,' she said, laughing as she kissed him. The children groaned.

'It's a bit early for that,' James said moodily. Laura and David laughed his comment off and carried on swaying to the music as he sang the words from the song to her. Their father singing was too much for the children to bear, and pulling faces they left the kitchen table and went back up to their rooms.

'They'll understand when they're in love,' David said.

'I only hope they'll be as lucky as we are,' Laura said.

'I don't think anyone could be as lucky as we are,' he'd said, nuzzling her throat as she laughed.

***

He passed the time waiting to see the doctor by flicking through women's magazines.

'Mr Peterson, Dr Jacob will see you now.' He dropped the magazine back on the pile and made his way to the doctor's room.

'Hi David,' the doctor said shaking his hand 'it's been a while.' David sat down.

'What seems to be the problem?' the doctor asked, pulling up David's file on his computer.

'I think I've got an ulcer,' David said as he explained his symptoms to the doctor.

'How long has this been going on?' the doctor asked.

'Past couple of months – although it's getting more frequent now and a bit more painful.'

'I see, can you take your shirt off and pop up on the table for me?' David did as he was told and lay on the bed. 'Tell me if it becomes painful,' he said as he started to feel around David's abdomen. Seated back at the desk the doctor began typing on his computer. 'I'd like to send you for a scan at the hospital, David.'

'Can't you just give me something to ease the pain?' David said, a bit surprised.

'I'd rather get you checked out properly before I start prescribing you pills.'

'I don't hold out much hope in getting an appointment anytime soon,' David said.

'It's okay, you'll be seen today – I'll phone ahead and let them know you're on your way.'

'Is everything alright?' David asked, concerned. This seemed to be a lot of effort for a simple ulcer.

'I'm sure you'll be fine,' the doctor said reassuringly. 'Like I said, it's just a precaution.' The two men stood up and shook hands. 'I'll call you when I *get the results back,' the doctor said, 'it might take a couple of weeks.'*

It had not been more than two days since David received a call from his Doctor requesting him to return to the hospital for immediate consultation. Upon entering the office David was instantly recognized and ushered into the consultant's room.

'David.' The consultant held out his hand and shook it gravely.

'This looks serious,' David joked, disconcerted by the look on the man's face. The consultant nodded.

'It is. I'm sorry David, there's no easy way to tell you.'

'Tell me what?' David asked, as his eyes frantically flickered from the notes on the desk to the consultant.

'You have liver cancer,' he said gently. 'It's spread to the surrounding organs and it's too far advanced for anything to be done.'

David felt the earth move beneath him. Feeling light-headed, he held onto the side of a chair to steady himself. Dumbfounded, he shook his head in disbelief.

'So it's not an ulcer?' he asked. The consultant shook his head sadly.

'How... how long?' he couldn't bring himself to say the words.

'Months,' the consultant said. 'Six at the most,' he added.

'I see, and what about chemotherapy?' David said desperately as his voice began to breakup.

'It's an option, but it will only prolong the inevitable for a short time and it has side-effects which can make you feel very ill,' he said, banishing the last glimmer of hope. 'Do you want me to call somebody?'

'Yes, yes, please call my wife,' David said, his

voice breaking with emotion as he wrote down her number. The consultant picked up the phone and was about to dial when David grabbed the phone. 'No... it's fine, don't tell her, I'll tell her,' he said backing off towards the door.

'Make another appointment at the reception on your way out and we'll discuss your options and what care you will need. Give yourself some time to take it all in David, it's a big shock.'

David turned and stumbled out of the door, passing the reception area and out onto the street. Nothing had changed on the outside. Nobody knew that he was dying; that he would be dead in a few months. He started to cry. Passers-by stepped out of his way, avoiding him like the plague. A man in a suit crying in the middle of the street in broad daylight was unthinkable.

Tears streaking down his face, he walked into the shop and bought a bottle of whiskey. He didn't know how he ended up on Bournemouth Pier, but he spent many hours there watching the swell of the waves come gently onto the shore. His mind wandering hopelessly into the waves one minute, and then slamming into the shore of reality the next. How was he going to tell Laura? She wouldn't be strong enough to handle this; he knew how hard her father's death was on her. What would happen to James and Emily? What about his dreams of fulfilling his lifelong ambition to travel the world? To grow old with Laura? He knew in his heart of hearts that he couldn't tell her. That he couldn't be the one to break her – nor could he be the one to mend her. He fumbled for his phone in his pocket and through glazed eyes texted Laura that he would be home late as he had an emergency meeting to attend to. Seconds later, his phoned beeped with a message of love from her.

He walked the short distance to the train station and half an hour later he was on the train to London. By the time he arrived, it was dark and the temperature had dropped. Still holding his bottle of courage, he rang the doorbell twice and was relieved when he heard footsteps. The door swung open and a woman stood there, clearly shocked by both his dishevelled appearance and seeing him on her doorstep.

'Sarah,' he managed to say before falling to his knees and crying like he'd never cried before. She knelt down beside him, taken aback by the stench of alcohol.

'David?' she said, rubbing his back.

He was mumbling incoherently.

'I don't know what to do, I don't know what to do.'

Using all the strength she had, she half dragged, half pulled him up and led him into the house. She guided him to a chair where he immediately flopped down and covered his face with one hand, still holding on to the whiskey with the other.

'David, unless you tell me what's wrong, I can't help you,' she said softly. 'Is there something wrong with Laura or the kids?'

He shook his head.

Relieved, she pushed on. 'Is it something to do with the business?'

Again, he shook his head.

'It's me,' he said, barely audible. Sarah hoped David hadn't come all this way to tell her of an extra-marital affair.

He looked up at her, his eyes bloodshot and pitiful.

'I'm dying Sarah, I'm fucking dying! I have liver cancer,' he said before breaking down again.

Sarah sat there, dumbfounded. She quickly moved to his side and held him, taking his head into her arms and crying silently with him. She gently rocked him until his tears subsided.

'I need your help,' he said, trying to sound stronger.

'Anything David, just ask.'

'I need you to come back to Bournemouth,' he said, knowing it was a mammoth favour he was asking her. 'I need you to be there for Laura.'

'Of course I will. How is she taking it?'

'She doesn't know and I'm not going to tell her,' he said. 'I know you think it's the wrong thing for me to do, but she isn't strong enough for this, I can't be a pillar of strength for both of us. I've only got a few months left, there's so much to do.'

'Okay,' she said without hesitation. 'It won't take me that long to pack a few things for the next few days. I can get the rest of my stuff moved up at the weekend. What you need to do,' she said taking the bottle from his hand, 'is drink a very strong black coffee and sober up; you don't want to be going home in this state.'

She disappeared into the kitchen, returning a few seconds later with a steaming mug of deep, rich smelling coffee. He took the coffee gratefully from her.

'I have a call to make and then we'll leave. I'll book into a hotel tonight and find somewhere to rent tomorrow.' Before she left the room, she turned to him. 'David.' He looked up at her. 'I'm truly sorry,' she said before vanishing from the doorway.

The next hour had been a daze. David had fallen asleep on the sofa. He had heard female voices speaking in hushed tones in the passage, before he felt his arm being shaken.

'David,' Sarah said gently, 'let's go.' Eyes half-opened, he had clumsily followed her out of the house into the car. The last thing he remembered was the

sound of the car door being shut behind him, and then he passed out. Although he was not fully sober, by the time they reached Bournemouth he was able to walk up and let himself in his front door. Sarah sat in the darkness after she watched him go inside. Tears slowly slid down her face as her emotions began to run wild.

Why is this happening? she thought to herself. Because life is about suffering. She nodded to the imaginary voice in her head.

'You're damn right about that,' she said out loud with an air of despair and drove off into the night.

David had called her the next morning. He had the worst hangover of his adult life and was still numb by the news of only having a few months to live. Looking at him, you would have thought he would live forever. He told her that Laura would be taking James and Emily to the climbing centre later that day and that would present the perfect opportunity for them to accidently bump into her.

'I've got to go, I've got another call coming through, I'll speak to you in a little while,' he said as he switched calls.

'David speaking,' he said into the mouthpiece.

'Hi David, I hope you don't mind me calling, I was given your number by your consultant,' a softly spoken woman's voice said. 'I'm a counsellor, I just wanted to touch base and let you know that you can reach me at any time to talk. My name is Sally.'

24

Laura calmly returned the telephone receiver to its cradle and got out of bed. Her mind was reeling as she tried to make sense of what she had just been told. She counted to ten in her head, trying to block out the waves of emotions that were overtaking her. She picked up the phone and pressed redial. Several seconds later Sarah answered the phone and she tried to talk but no words came out. Her throat tightened. She could hear Sarah calling her name but it seemed as if she was calling from a distance. The last thing she heard was Sarah saying that she was making her way over and then the phone went dead.

Everything from then on was in a state of slow flux. Sarah and Jada arriving at her front door. Jada going into the house to look after the children. Laura being led down the path by Sarah and helping her into her car. Driving through the quiet streets and ending up at the Royal something hospital.

Sally was waiting at the entrance to the hospital.

'I'm sorry to rush you Laura, but there really isn't much time,' she said, urgently leading her through the maze of corridors until they reached the Intensive Care Ward. A nurse with a kindly face and compassionate eyes met Laura at the entrance to the ward. Her muffled voice reached Laura despite the dark fog her mind had become.

'Come with me dear, he has been calling for you. I'm sorry but I don't think he will be with us for much longer, we are just keeping him comfortable now.'

The words hurtled towards her like a bullet fired from a gun, straight into her heart. She wanted to dodge them as they echoed through her head. As much as she willed her legs to move, they would not. Just when she thought she could not stand it another moment, she felt the comforting arm of Sarah circling her waist. Gratitude washed through her veins. She could not have faced this alone. To Laura the place looked like a living morgue.

'He needs you,' Sarah said softly into Laura's ear.

Each bed was surrounded with machines, and various medical devices were connected to unconscious patients. Alarms went off in the background as nurses and doctors were alerted to someone's needs. The incessant whooshing of respirators filled the air, figures in white coats moved quietly between the beds, checking on the still bodies which lay beneath stark white sheets. Hushed conversations took place between nurses stationed by a desk.

As she approached the bed the full horror of the situation hit her and she began to cry. Tears streamed down her face, magnifying and distorting everything she saw into a hazy blur. She stood staring at him, trembling on the edge of hysteria. He was wearing an oxygen mask so she could only see the top part of his face. He was still there, but he was a different man, yellow, frail, a shadow of his former self. She felt an eerie sensation of being cut off from time, space and the rest of the world. Could she have only known that David was at the end of his life for the past twenty minutes? She felt Sarah at her side, her arm around her shoulder, coaxing her towards the bed. When she reached it, Laura took his bony hand gently in hers.

'I'm here, David,' she said close to his ear, trying to be strong for him, but failing miserably. She could not stop the avalanche of tears cascading down her face. 'I'm here,' she repeated, barely getting the words out. 'I love you so much David, I love you so much,' she said, wanting to hold him tightly but afraid she would crush his frail bones. He suddenly opened his eyes. For one split second, she saw David, the man she grew to love and cherish. With his free hand, he weakly removed the oxygen mask from his face and in the corner of his eyes tears began to glisten.

'I'm so sorry, Laura. I love you more than you'll ever know,' he said faintly and then he closed his eyes again. His breathing became laboured, a final sound gurgled up from his throat and then he was gone. Never to awaken again, never hold her, tell her he loved her or make her laugh only the way he could. He had stepped beyond the boundaries of his life. His pain and suffering was now over, he was at peace; however she felt like hers had just begun. She fought the urge to start screaming hysterically, to beg him to come back, not to leave her. Instead she sat by his bedside holding his lifeless hand in hers, willing him to know how much she loved him and that where ever he had gone he had taken her soul with him.

She went through the following week with a mute detachment. She played the words that Dr Leigh had instilled in her repeatedly in her mind, *'Stay in the present moment... Accept death as the natural process of life'*. She hung on to reality with urgent desperation. She somehow managed to collect the death certificate, arrange the funeral, order the flowers and hire the caterers for the wake. Joe had been a reassuring presence despite his despicable behaviour the last time they met.

'I just can't believe he didn't tell me,' he cried, 'he didn't tell anyone, how could he have carried that knowledge around with him and not told anyone.'

'It was his way of protecting us all, as silly as it sounds, he thought he was doing the right thing,' Laura said mournfully.

I don't want you to worry about the business Laura, I will take care of everything for you, just let me know when you want to come in and sort out your affairs,' he said.

'I will, in a little while' she had said.

On the day of the funeral, conversations had filtered off her in hopeless, futile sparks. James and Emily had been inconsolable as their father was laid to rest.

'I know you don't want to hear this right now but I'm here for you and the children, it's what David wanted,' she said with compassion.

'Thank you Sally, I will be in touch,' Laura promised.

Although something had irreparably broken within them all, she made a promise to herself that she would help James and Emily get through the dark days that lay ahead. Not fall apart as her mother had, how - she did not know.

'What am I supposed to do? I don't know what to do,' Laura said to no one in particular. She was seated by the window with Sarah in a bistro overlooking the sea. The Earl Grey tea in the white porcelain cups remained untouched.

'You don't have to do anything,' Sarah said.

'The kids need me...' she countered. It was more of an assertion than a question.

'Laura, you'll get through this, you're stronger than you think,' Sarah said. There was a long silence before Laura looked at her friend with confusion in her eyes.

'Why didn't you tell me Sarah? Why didn't you tell me so we could have spent what precious time he had left, together?'

'Because he asked me not to, he had his reasons,' she added. 'Do you really think you would have wanted to know? Hand on heart,' she asked her softly.

'No,' she said, feeling somewhat ashamed of her weakness, 'I think it would have been worse for him as well. He would never have been able to do the things he wanted to do - things that were so precious to him in the end. I would have just hindered him with my worrying.'

'James and Emily had the best of him Laura. He didn't want them to see him like he was, he didn't want to scar them. He didn't want them to grow up like he did when his dad died.'

'I know, that was David though, always putting everyone above himself.'

'He had faith in you - don't let him down now, let him live on in your memory and be strong like he knew you would.'

'I will,' Laura sniffed. And it would take time, but that moment was a turning point for her. She inhaled deeply and made up her mind there and then that she would follow her dream, just as David would have wanted her too.

***

As Laura let herself into her house, she was puzzled by the silence. Sarah had said she would pick up James and Emily from school and drop them home. She walked into the kitchen feeling a little disappointed when the earth shattering scream startled her so much that she fell back against the door.

'Surprise!' they all shouted in unison. She was shocked to see her mother and stepfather who must have travelled all the way from Australia. Sarah, Jada, Joe and many of the friends she had made at college were also there to her surprise. She'd wondered why no one wanted to celebrate the end of their course and now she knew why; they were all in the surprise party themselves!

'Congratulations,' her mother said, walking up to her and holding her tightly. Through tears, she whispered in her ear, 'I'm so very proud of you Laura, we both are.' She stepped aside so her husband could hold his stepdaughter. Crying, Laura hugged him back and caught Sarah's attention.

'I'm going to kill you,' she mouthed, and then she blew her friend a kiss of enormous gratitude.

'How does it feel to be a real journalist, Mum?' Emily asked, wrapping her arms around her.

'Just great!' she said, bending over to kiss her head.

When everyone had left and the children were finally in bed, Laura sat with Sarah and Jada in front of the roaring fire. Sarah quietly disappeared and came back with a beautifully wrapped box.

'You've already given me a present,' Laura protested as Sarah handed it to her.

'It's not from me,' Sarah said with a smile. Laura looked puzzled.

'Then who's it from?' she asked, removing the wrapping paper. She gasped as she saw it was a state of the art *Nixon D1* Camera. 'Who on earth would have bought me this, it costs a fortune!' she said, thinking that it must have come from her parents.

Opening the card on top, she immediately recognised the handwriting. She pressed the card to her mouth, tears falling down her face. *He* had been the one who had ordered her the college brochure – it hadn't been just a coincidence. *He knew me so well,* she thought, smiling between tears. She slowly savoured the last words he had ever written to her; she would treasure them forever.

Laura
I hear this camera is what all the top
photojournalists use.
I knew you could do it!
Wherever I am, know that I am so proud of you.
I will love you forever.
David

Printed in Great Britain
by Amazon